The Other Side of Her Storm

A Novel

Bridget L. Rose

First Edition – 2025

Editing: Bridget L. Rose Books Inc.

Cover Design: Bridget L. Rose Books Inc.

Formatting: Bridget L. Rose Books Inc.

Illustrations 1+3: @emilyxvrs

Illustration 2: @irdeinfierno

Trigger Warnings

This book contains explicit sex scenes, as well as MotoGP crashes which might be scary for some readers and vulgar language. It contains topics of grief, anxiety and mental health, and more that may be triggering for some readers.

Author's Note

This novella takes place shortly after the end of Chase: Part One & Two.

This novella is heavier on the MotoGP racing so just be aware of that.

This novella also contains a lot of fluff and no conflict in their marriage, however, there is outside drama to keep things interesting!

Other than that, I hope you enjoy this novella!

MotoGP

Teams Series

Hawkes
CWM MOTOGP

PRIMA PANTERA
MOTOGP TEAM

FUOCO MOTOGP

SATURN RACING TEAM

Black Widow
Racing

zeitgeist racing
MOTOGP Team

MotoGP

Teams Series

CLOVER RACING

TRIANGLE RACING
MOTOGP TEAM

MARIPOSA MOTOGP

LÖWE RACING

PHOENIX RACING
MOTOGP TEAM

Race Schedule

Thailand: February 27–March 2

Argentina: March 14–16

USA: March 28–30

Qatar: April 11–13

Spain: April 25–27

France: May 9–11

United Kingdom: May 23–25

Aragon: June 6–8

Italy: June 20–22

Netherlands: June 27–29

Germany: July 11–13

Czechia: July 18–20

Austria: August 15–17

Hungary: August 22–24

Catalonia: September 5–7

San Marino: September 12–14

Japan: September 26–28

Indonesia: October 3–5

Australia: October 17–19

Malaysia: October 24–26

Portugal: November 7–9

Valencia: November 14–16

This book is dedicated to everyone who is looking for the other side of the storm. I promise, the dark clouds will part to let sunshine filter into your life, creating the most beautiful rainbow. Be patient, and your arcoíris will find you, just like mine found me.

— Julián "Storm" Alvarez

This book is dedicated to my number one Julián fan, my sister. I hope you'll stop annoying me for another book on him now.

This is a continuation of Scarlette and Julián's story from *The Inside of a Rainbow.*

Make sure to read their full-length novel first before you read this novella.

You can find all the translations of the Spanish words and phrases in the back of the book.

Chapter 1

Julián

My rainbow and I didn't have a fancy wedding.

We didn't invite a hundred people to witness our ceremony.

She didn't want that, and I've always wanted whatever she does.

And I'm so glad it went exactly the way it did because I dream of that day every night.

The day I married the love of my life with the promise of forever on our side.

I'm nervous.

Fuck, I've never been so nervous.

Scarlette Roots is the love of my life, the reason I breathe, my everything, and if she hates the suit and tie I've chosen for our special day, I might actually drive my bike off a cliff.

"I know not smiling is your thing and all, but today is your wedding day. You can look happy, you know?" Elias says, but I simply shake my head at him because even

if I wanted to, even though the guilt I've been carrying because of Jamie has eased immensely since I met Scarlette, I can't bring myself to do anything but frown.

"My hands are sweating, breathing is difficult, and my head is spinning. I don't need to smile. I need to sit down," I say, a shaky breath slipping past my lips as I brush a hand down my suit. "You think Scar will like this color tie? I know you chose it and told me to trust you, but I really don't," I explain, and when I catch Elias' jaw dropping in offense, I almost crack a smile.

Almost.

"You can be a real dick."

"Hey, this is my wedding day. You're supposed to be nice to me," I remind him, allowing this conversation to distract me from the fact that I'm scared my beautiful woman will have changed her mind about spending the rest of her life with me.

"I have been nice to you. I became your best man and I got you an amazing gift off the registry you didn't ask to have made but I created for you anyway."

My mouth clamps shut because he's making a lot of good points. My nervousness returns tenfold, and I have to sit down to keep my legs from giving out.

"What if she changed her mind?" I ask, covering my mouth once the words have left it. Elias squats down in front of me, placing a comforting hand on my knee.

"She hasn't. Scarlette loves you so much, Storm. One might even say that she loves you more than anyone has ever loved their partner, the only exceptions being you and me."

His words settle the turmoil inside of me a little, but until I see Scarlette, I won't be able to be calmed fully. We've been apart for less than twenty-four hours because she didn't want to risk us having bad luck by seeing each other before the wedding—her superstition, not mine because I want to see her every single second of the day, no matter what she does—but it feels like forever ago since I laid my eyes on her.

"It's almost time. You can almost see her," Elias assures me when I don't respond to his previous statement, too lost in my head.

"How much longer?" I ask, hope blooming in my chest. It's barely enough to drown out the uncomfortable feeling of panic camping in there.

"Ten minutes."

I nod several times, standing up and stepping in front of the mirror. I smooth out my lavender-colored tie, trusting Elias' judgment. He said she would love it, and considering most of her closet has lavender-colored clothing and that she always smells like lavender, I know he's right.

My suit, dress shirt, and shoes are entirely black, so the splash of color from the tie brightens up my look a little. I don't want Scarlette to think I'm stuck in darkness today when I've never been happier. In reality, my darkness is nowhere to be found. Not when the woman who brings all colors of the rainbow into my life is about to become my wife.

"Five minutes," Elias says once I've adjusted my hair several more times, obsessively smoothed out my tie again, and made sure my cufflinks are still where they're supposed to be.

Scar gave them to me a year ago, when I had to attend a boring directors' meeting at my dad's company. The cufflinks are in the shape of airplanes, a little something to keep my father close to me today. I stare at them for a moment, blinking away the pain of his death that hasn't stopped haunting me since he passed away.

I wish he was here today. I wish he could see me marry my happy ending, the one he always hoped I'd find one day.

Tears blur my vision, but I swallow them down successfully.

At least until Mamá walks in and my emotions flood my chest all over again as tears drop down her cheeks.

"Mijo, te ves muy guapo," *she says and covers her mouth, letting more tears fall. My own follow soon after.*

"Gracias, *Mamá*. Tú también," *I say and attempt a small smile, but it still feels so very unnatural to give it to anyone but Scar, so I don't bother trying.*

"Your father would be so proud of you. Today. And every day before and after, too. He was always proud of the man you were, but he'd be even more so of the man you've become."

Mamá smoothes out my suit jacket, a sad smile stretching her lips. She may have a complicated relationship with my biological father, one I don't agree with in the slightest, but that man means nothing to me, so I know she doesn't mean him. Mamá will never refer to the man who abandoned me.

No.

She means the man who spent my entire life teaching me everything there is to know about the world, and even when I didn't agree with him on things, I learned important lessons. Like you don't have to love everything about a person in order to always want them to be close to you. You don't have to have everything figured out at a certain point in your life, even when society tells you you have to. Love can get you through anything, even the darkest and toughest times.

"If you continue talking about him, I won't be able to stop crying, Mamá," I say with a stern look, warning her to drop this conversation unless she wants me to be an emotional mess in the corner and miss out on the best day of my life.

"I had to say my piece. He would have wanted me to remind you," she says, and I pull her into a hug, kissing her forehead.

It took us a while to get back here after everything that happened, but I'm glad we're on good terms again. I love my mother with my whole heart and fighting with her brought me nothing but pain.

Unnecessary pain.

"Ready?" she asks, pulling me out of my thoughts once more.

"Words cannot describe how ready I am to marry the love of my life," I reply, my heart palpitating at the mere thought of seeing Scarlette soon.

Mamá and Elias walk me to the little makeshift altar that I built for today. We're getting married in the yard of the house we've been living in together for a year now. She moved in with me the day Elias moved in with Violet, and I had never been as happy as I was then when I saw Scarlette's things slowly taking over every inch of the house. She made it a true home with her very presence, and seeing her walk around in nothing but a shirt and underwear, watching her dance barefoot around the living room, all of it had—has—me desperately in love with the idea of spending the rest of my life with her.

We invited no one to the ceremony except for Halo fucking Henderson—who I hate a lot less now than I did when I saw him kissing Scar years ago—who is marrying us today. He got his license specifically for today, and I know it makes my woman happy to have her friend here. She didn't invite her parents because she didn't want them to find ways to ruin the day for her, and even though I know her mother will make her feel guilty for the rest of her life when she finds out, today isn't about her self-centered mother or abusive father. Today is about Scar, and a little bit about me, and I want nothing to ruin it for either of us.

Clearly, neither does she, or she would have invited her parents.

"Thank you for being here," I tell Halo, who gives me one of his easy-going smiles.

"A pleasure. While I was always hoping she'd choose me in the end, I can't deny you're the better choice of partner. You certainly love her more than anyone ever could," he says and nudges me with his shoulder, still grinning brightly.

"It's a good thing you ended your speech the way you did or I'd have knocked you on your ass."

I may not have to be jealous anymore, not the way I was when Scar and I were fake dating, but that doesn't change the possessiveness I feel when it comes to my wife. She's everything to me, and I'm going to make sure she never forgets that I want her above everything else. A bit of possessiveness is most certainly a good way to show her that I will only ever have eyes for her. That I'd fight anyone who tried to take her from me.

"I know," is Halo's only response, but he chuckles, too, and all I manage to do is shake my head at him.

All words die out as soon as music starts playing and Violet walks down the "aisle," if you can even call it that, with flower petals falling from her fingers. She's carrying a tiny basket that she's taking them out of, and I watch her impatiently, wishing she'd hurry up so I can see Scar.

Luckily, I don't have to wait long.

But I could have used another few minutes to prepare because the sight of mi arcoíris, *almost brings me to my fucking knees.*

Her dress is flawless. It is the same lavender color as my tie—I should have really trusted Elias—with an off-shoulder cut but sleeves that hug three-fourths of her arms. Her breasts are pushed up by a corset that has lots of lavender embroidered on it, and the train of it, flowing effortlessly behind her, has the same design. The rest of her dress is flowy and looks simply devastating on her.

I would have expected her to use makeup to cover up her scar a little in the way she often does on special occasions, since it's a memory she doesn't like to remember, but today, it's fully on display. It makes her look even more beautiful to me, which is saying a lot. She's placed bits of lavender in the sections of her hair that are braided, her curvy body is perfectly on display in that dress, and her blue eyes are almost sparkling with joy as she takes me in. There's not much that could make her look more beautiful than she does at this moment.

I suck in a sharp breath, not preventing the tears from shooting into my eyes at the sight of her walking toward me. A smile covers my whole face when I notice hers, and I don't even think twice about letting it. Scar is carrying the bundle of lavender I handed Violet this morning to give to her, our tradition still very much alive and thriving. I give her a bundle almost weekly, even if we're apart. And every time the bundles are about to wither, we turn them into oil she can put on her skin.

"You look like a dream, love. A gorgeous, stunning, breathtaking, devastating dream," I say as soon as she's close enough. I place an arm around her and pull her in, reveling in the warmth spreading through my chest when she giggles right before I place my mouth on hers.

Scar's fingers slide up my chest, wrapping around my lapels to pull me closer and deepen the kiss. Halo lets out a low whistle, and I know Elias would have probably done the same if Halo hadn't beaten him to it. I keep smiling against Scar's lips, unable to hold it back when I've never been so happy in my entire life.

"You're going to have to stop kissing her if you want to get married," Violet reminds us, and Scar steps back, but I follow her like I can't quite get enough of her.

Well, I can't *get enough of her.*

The entire time Halo speaks, I stare at Scarlette. I study her face, barely registering the words until he turns to me and allows me to finally say the vows I didn't have to write down.

The words have been written on my heart since I met her.

"Scarlette, you are all the beautiful colors in the world. You are the light in my darkness, the very reason I'm alive. Because I know I was made to worship you. I was made to do everything in my power to bring you happiness. That is my life's purpose. You are my life's purpose." Tears fall down her cheeks, but I catch them, completely ignoring the single one running down my own. "My heart has been yours for years. It'll be yours until it stops beating. You are my priority for everything in life, and you

always will be. Without you, my success would be meaningless. Without you, my life would be empty. Without you, mi arcoíris, I'd be eternally lost. So, I want to tie myself to you forever. I want to be with you through everything, the good and the bad. I want to spend every second I have left being your husband. I love you so much, Scar. You're the love of my life."

Scar covers her mouth to hold back a sob, but I grab her hands in mine as I say the last sentence of my vows.

"Quiero ser tu todo, arcoíris, para siempre."

She shakes her head as her shoulders shake with a silent sob, but I don't blame her. I'm crying, too. Fuck, I'm crying in front of everyone, and I can't quite bring myself to care. I never thought I'd find her. I never thought she'd want me too. I always hoped I would, I'm a romantic at heart after all, but finding the love of your life, your soulmate, seems like something many people will not experience in their lives. But I did. I found her, she found me, and she's choosing me in this life.

"For someone as quiet and broody as you, you sure know how to turn the words in the English and Spanish languages into something beautiful," Halo says, staring up into the bright-blue sky as if trying to keep tears at bay.

"Are you crying?" Scar asks him, but he pulls his lips into a firm line and shakes his head.

"Of course not."

He lets out a shaky laugh, then clears his throat. It's the first time I flash him somewhat of a grin because I'm finding his reaction to my vows too amusing not to. He's still too busy trying to keep back his tears to pay me any attention.

"Your turn, Scarlette," Halo says, nodding her way. I notice she's silently laughing at her friend, but when she turns to face me, her blue eyes finding mine, her expression softens. It's still pure sunshine, blinding in a wonderful sort of way.

"I don't think my vows will be as amazing as yours, but I will give it my best shot," she says with a little giggle, a sound so soft it travels through my entire system before settling in my chest. "Julián, breaking through your stormy walls and getting to know the man you are deep inside has been my favorite accomplishment in life so far. You are my favorite person in the entire world, and if I could, I'd spend every day with you by my side. That feeling hasn't changed in the years we've been dating. That feeling isn't going to change for me because that's how much I love you. Yes, we need our space, but by the end of it, I always want to be with you. And that's why I know you're the love of my life, too. You are my Storm."

"Actually, I called him Storm fir—" I cut Elias off before he can finish that sentence.

"Shut the fuck up before I put tape on your mouth." My voice is low and threatening, and he chuckles as he lifts his hands in mock surrender. "Please keep going, my love," I say and squeeze Scar's hands. She's grinning at me, not in the least bit bothered by the interruption.

"You are my anchor in the darkness. You are the oxygen in my lungs when I can't breathe during an anxiety attack. You are everything I have ever needed. I can't wait to spend the rest of my life with you, calling you my husband and hearing you call me your wife."

As soon as I'm sure she's finished speaking, I pull her in for another kiss. This time, Halo mumbles something about declaring us husband and wife, but I'm not listening to him anymore. Scar is my wife, even without someone saying she is, and if he has to go through that whole thing to make it official on paper, so be it. That doesn't mean I have to waste a second listening to him when I could be kissing Scar, though.

My wife melts into me for several seconds before pulling away to hug Violet, Elias, Mamá, and Halo, and then pulling me toward the front of our house. We have a plane to catch, a honeymoon to go on, and our family members know that. They knew we'd only stay long enough to be married—Mamá made us compromise from getting married at City Hall to having a ceremony in the backyard—and we're not wasting another second starting our new life.

On the rear of her motorcycle are two cans attached, the same as on mine, and Elias had license plates made that read "Just" and "Married" so that as we drive through Moonville on our way to the airport, people can see them. Our luggage and bags have already been brought to the airport as well, perks of having a private jet thanks to my father's millions, so all we need to bring is ourselves. Not even bothering to change her dress, only her shoes, Scar runs to her bike, pulling her helmet on. I shake my head with a smile as I do the same, and soon, we're off, riding down the highway.

I watch her dress fly in the wind, short enough not to get stuck in her wheel or endanger her in any way. No. I don't have to worry. I simply get to admire the way she looks, freshly married to me, doing one of things she loves most in the world: being on her bike while we ride together.

I speed up to go right beside her, pointing at my chest, making half a heart with my hand, and then pointing at her.

I love you.

She does it back, then zooms down the highway.

I don't hesitate to chase after her.

JUST
MARRIED

CHAPTER 2

Julián

"What the fuck do you mean the company is in debt? My father had *billions*," I say, my heart all the way in my stomach. I've been forced to attend a stupid board meeting again, but this time I'm almost glad they called me because if I had heard this from Elias on a random day with no context, I think my head would have exploded.

"A deal went bad and we—" Elias is cut off by another board member, and I almost fire him on the spot.

"Elias fucked up. He invested too much money in more environmentally friendly solutions for the company, and they've been draining the accounts while clients started leaving because of them. We've been leaking money for years." The bald man,, whose name I cannot remember for the life of me, shoots my best friend an evil look that makes me want to strangle him.

"Get out," I say, looking at him.

"What?" he asks, perplexed by my harsh tone and words.

"Get out. Your tone is not appreciated in this meeting." I shift my gaze to the door, a clear indication of what I want him to do. He gathers his things and leaves without another word, a smart decision on his part.

I've been a silent owner since I put Elias in charge three years ago. I wanted nothing to do with it, but I also didn't have the heart to sell my father's life's work, so I became the owner who stayed out of the business until absolutely necessary.

This qualifies as absolutely necessary.

"Elias, talk to me. How much do we owe?" I ask, not caring how we got to this point. It doesn't matter if it's his fault—which it doesn't sound like it is, since he's simply trying to clean up the company and make it better for the world—what matters is finding a solution.

"About three million," he says, avoiding eye contact with me.

"Fuck," I mumble as I deflate in my seat, getting extremely irritated with the thing because it rolls backward.

Who the fuck thought I needed a chair with fucking wheels?

Okay, I might be more upset about the company being in debt than I ever thought I would be. I hated this company for so long. I thought my father was greedy for making so much money and keeping it all for himself, but now, with Elias in charge, it's accomplishing so much good in the world already.

"I'm so sorry, Storm, I thought things would turn around, that we would find investors, but shit hit the fan, and now we're in debt," Elias explains, but I'm barely paying attention. I stare blankly at the other head of the table, where my father used to sit, and I wonder what he'd say if he was here right now.

I can picture him sitting there, disappointment on his face. There would be disapproval in his gaze, but he wouldn't say anything. He'd let me see it, let me know I've made all the wrong decisions for his business. I can picture him staring at me expectantly, waiting for me to come up with a solution to the problem. I have none.

I'm not a business person.

He was.

Elias is.

But my best friend is as lost as I am right now.

The mere imaginary sight of him has a tsunami of emotion hitting my chest, drowning all of my organs in sorrow.

Panic and pain slither around my throat, and I push away from the table, suddenly grateful for those stupid wheels because they make the motion smoother. I'm on my feet a second later, reaching for the knot of my tie. My fingers fumble with it until I'm able to pull it down. At the same time, my feet bring me to the door of the meeting room, and I rush through it, ignoring the ten sets of eyes on me.

I have to get out, away from everything that reminds me of the man who raised me, but is no longer by my side.

This is my father's legacy.

Everything he's built is on the line.

"Ahhh," I let out when the breath in my lungs start burning from how shallowly I'm breathing.

Only once I reach the roof of the building do I manage to take a deep breath. I pull at my tie knot again, opening it all the way and letting either side dangle down my chest. I unbutton the first two buttons of my dress shirt and take another deep breath.

In.

Hold.

And out, just like my wife taught me.

The cold air helps shock my system enough to allow my brain to refocus, from the panic to shivering from the icy wind. It's sunny outside, but not even the sun is making the winter any more bearable here in Moonville.

"Fuck."

I lean against the railing, taking several more deep breaths until the panic subsides enough to allow my head to start spiraling in the right direction.

Down the tunnel of options to save my father's company.

I will not let him down. I can't. Even if I wanted nothing to do with this company, this is his legacy.

How could I ever let it die if there is an option to save it?

"Storm, man, I'm so sorry," Elias says, his voice pulling me into reality. I tilt my head his way, taking in his furrowed brows and frown.

Ever since Violet went into the third trimester of her pregnancy, he's been sleeping less because his wife has been sleeping less. He looks exhausted, with dark circles under his eyes, and his hair always a mess from running his fingers through it absentmindedly. I've never wanted children. Looking at Elias, whose baby is not even born, I'm even surer.

Scar, being my soulmate in every way possible, also doesn't want children, which is why three years ago, I got a vasectomy to make sure she can stop taking the birth control that she never wanted to take in the first place. Now, we get to spend the rest of our lives being the fun uncle and aunt who have lots of dogs, cats, and whatever else Scar wants without her having to be negatively impacted by birth control and either of us having to worry about any unwanted surprises.

"Stop apologizing. It's not going to help anything," I say and try to soften my gaze enough to show him I'm not angry with him but the situation.

"But I feel horrible," he explains, so I take a step toward him, then another, until I'm able to place a comforting hand on his shoulder.

"I know you do, and I wish I could make you feel less so, *hermano*, but until we find a solution to the company being in debt, there is nothing I can say to help you."

Over the years, I've grown a lot when it comes to opening up and talking to Elias. It used to be harder for me. Sharing my feelings was always extremely uncomfortable, but since Scar came into my life, I've realized I have to work harder to make relationships work. There is no avoiding communication if I want a healthy relationship with the people I love.

"What solution? Another deal? Storm, I've tried. I have tried everything, but people don't want this company's highly priced products when they used to be much cheaper."

"Cheaper and more damaging to the environment." Elias frowns at me.

"Yeah, but what does the environment matter to greedy people who want to keep getting richer and richer?" he asks, silencing me. "What can I do to fix this?" my best friend asks, and I shake my head at him, squeezing his shoulder one more time.

"Nothing. At least not yet. Let me go home and speak to my wife. She's smart enough to come up with a solution within minutes," I say, and Elias chuckles.

"You know you can say 'Scar,' right? I know her name."

"I know, but referring to her as 'my wife' is pure bliss, and I can't stop."

"So possessive," he mumbles, but throws me a wicked smile.

"Always."

I hate the winter here.

I hate the cold.

I hate that I can't ride my bike.

I hate it all.

What I don't hate is the way Scar sits in front of the fireplace, wrapped up in a blanket and one of my oversized hoodies. Seeing her in my clothing, the ring I gave her sparkling in the light of the fire, warms my chest in ways I'll never be able to understand. Her hair is braided into two Dutch braids, and she's snacking on some crackers she bought when we went grocery shopping yesterday.

As soon as her eyes catch me in the doorframe of our living room, a bright smile covers her face, making her glossy lips pull wide. During the winter, Scar always struggles with dry lips, so she puts on lots of balm or lip oil, making her lips look really fucking kissable.

"Welcome home, husband," she says, and I struggle to breathe as my knees turn to putty.

"*Hola, mi querida esposa*," I reply, taking several strides toward her until I'm in front of her.

She's still grinning until I'm close enough for her to see the tortured expression I'm most likely wearing.

Her face falls as I sink to my knees beside her.

"What happened?" she asks, removing her blanket to slide to the ground beside me. She cups my face, and for the first time since I found out what was happening with my dad's company, I feel at peace.

A breath whooshes out of me at the mere contact, her skin on mine, and I waste no time placing my forehead against Scar's, soaking in her comfort.

Once I've regained my voice, I tell her everything. I tell her about the debt the company is in, how lost I feel, the way the grief in my chest is making breathing more difficult, and the fear of letting my father down. Every single thought, feeling, and concern slips past my lips, but Scar never lets go of me. Her hands drop from my face to wrap around one of my hands, which she presses to her chest.

"I need your help. I need to find a solution," I say once I'm done, and her blue eyes scan my face before she falls into deep thought.

I don't rush her. I don't do anything but wait with my left hand, the one she isn't hugging to her chest, lifting to play with the strand of hair she purposely didn't braid so it could frame her face.

"How much money do you need to get the company back on track?" she asks, and I inhale deeply when the scent of her, of lavender, fills my nose.

"Three million, give or take," I reply, dropping my hand again to run it over her thick thigh.

God, I love her thighs.

I love that they could crush me easily.

I love that they are strong and carry my woman toward her dreams.

Most of all, I love them because they belong to Scar, and I love every part of her.

"Julián, you know what the solution is," my wife says, so I lift my gaze from admiring the cellulite on her legs back to her face.

"Kissing you until my problems vanish? Burying my face between your pretty legs until the rest of the world disappears? Slip inside you and lose myself to you in the way I always want to?" I ask, and Scar's cheeks immediately turn red as a shy smile curls her lips.

"Baby, be serious for a moment. You can get back to seducing me after we discuss how to save your father's company," she says and places her hand on my throat, keeping me back because I was leaning forward to kiss her.

"But I'd much rather seduce you. With my hands, or mouth, or words. You choose, love," I say, pressing forward and making her hand push harder against my throat. A thrill goes through me instantly.

"You have to become MotoGP champion, husband. This season, your first, you have to win that title and get the prize money. It'll be enough to save the company." The lust that was clouding my thoughts drifts away, leaving me to lean back as I plop onto my ass on the floor.

"That's not possible, *arcoíris*. I have years of experience racing motorcycles, sure, but not at a MotoGP level."

"That doesn't matter. You have the experience, and I will be your race engineer for this season. There is nothing that can stop us, not with you racing for Hawke, too."

My lips seal shut as I consider her words.

"That's a lot of pressure."

Scar crawls into my lap and grabs my face, making me look up at her. Her thumbs trace the apples of my cheeks, and my eyes flutter shut at the warmth and gentleness of her touch.

"We can carry it together," she says and kisses my lips softly and oh so gently. "It's the only way I can see the company getting out of debt," she adds, kissing me again.

It's difficult not to get entirely distracted with her mouth on mine.

"Okay," I say because I know she's right.

I know it's the only way *I*, the person without any business expertise, could get that kind of money. I got quite a big sum of money when I got my seat at Hawke CWM MotoGP, but not that much.

Scar's right, and there is no arguing with her just because I'm terrified I won't be good enough to accomplish such a huge thing. Because I'm terrified I'll let everyone down. There is no arguing when I don't want to think about any of this anymore. I just want to be with Scar.

"If I beg, will you take off your clothes?" I ask, bringing that shy smile back to her face.

"You don't have to beg, Julián. I'm more than happy to get naked for you." Her words are followed by her ripping my hoodie over her head, leaving her only in her panties in front of me.

"You're all I need to be at peace," I say as I lift my hands to cup her breasts, watching her smile down at me.

Then her mouth finds mine again, and every single worry in my life drifts right out of my body.

CHAPTER 3

Julián

My wife's moan is a special kind of drug for me.

I get so high off the sound, sometimes I forget where or even who I am. All that matters is getting another hit, and I'll only get it if I keep thrusting up inside of her, hitting her G-spot with every stroke.

My skin is on fire, but not because of the heat of the fireplace beside us.

No.

It's on fire because desire has taken over every inch of me, and I'm so hot because she feels so good. She looks so good. I'm in heaven.

"Yes, husband, right there," Scar moans, almost screams, and I thrust up into her, my head falling back as I groan in pleasure.

When I first met Scar, she had no experience with sex. She was shy and nervous, but now? Now she's adventurous, vocal, and fuck, she loves it when I tell her what to do. She loves being my good girl and obeying my commands because she knows they will lead her to have the most pleasure imaginable.

Which is why she doesn't hesitate when I say, "Get on your back for me, love. I need to go deeper." As much as I love her riding me, watching her perfect breasts and stomach bounce with my thrusts, I want to go deeper.

I need to.

Once she's on her back, I move to straddle one of her legs, placing the other around my stomach. I don't hesitate to slide back inside her, angling the leg that's wrapped around me up and back to sink as deep as I can.

"Fuuuuuuck," I groan once I'm all the way inside of her, and Scar lets out the most wonderful of moans that has my cock pulsing inside of her.

"Oh, yes. You're so deep," Scar moans, her hand reaching for me until she manages to slide her nails across my abdomen, leaving the faintest ache that spikes my pleasure higher. I thrust inside of her harder, angling her leg even further back.

I see stars the next time I drive into her, Scar squeezing around me as she shakes through her third orgasm of the night. I keep going, pushing her pleasure as far as it goes and dragging out her orgasm until she taps my stomach to tell me to slow down.

"Oh my God. Oh my God," she repeats several times, and I smile down at her, breathless but so incredibly happy. I lean down, both of my hands cupping her breasts as my mouth finds hers.

Scar lifts her head off the pillow I placed down earlier for when I was on my back, meeting my hungry kiss.

"Julián," she starts, but I bite her bottom lip in warning. "Husband," she corrects with a little laugh.

While we have sex, I'm either husband or baby. I insisted on it because, while not many people used to call me by my name, now that I'm in MotoGP, they do. And I want Scar to call me something special, something that's just hers.

Husband and baby both exclusively belong to her.

"You're still so hard. Please, I want to make you come," she says, sitting up even more to reach between us. Her fingers run along the area of my cock that isn't buried deep inside of her, and I shiver at the soft touch.

"How do you want to make me come?" I love playing this game with her. With every time that we do, she becomes more and more comfortable sharing her desires and fantasies with me as quickly as they come to mind.

"I want to suck you off while you lick my pussy," she says, and it takes all of my willpower not to come inside of her from nothing more than her words and the warmth of her pussy wrapped around me.

Good fucking God.

"I love your filthy mouth so much, *arcoíris,*" I say, stroking a hand down her leg. "Tell me why you want that," I say with a smirk, drawing out of her slowly just to push back inside her at the same pace.

I know the answer, but I love it when she talks dirty.

"Because you love fucking me with your mouth, and I love doing the same with you," she explains as she runs her hands over her breasts, arching her back when I push back inside.

"Damn right, love. For me, there's nothing better than tasting you, especially after you've already made a mess by coming on my cock and fingers. Gotta clean you up," I say as I pull out entirely and close the distance between us to place my tongue flat against her beautifully swollen clit.

"Baby, I—" She cuts off to whimper when I use the tip of my tongue to flick it over her clit. "I want you in my mouth," Scar pants out, but her fingers slip into my hair, tugging as she rolls her hips, chasing her pleasure.

Tearing myself off Scar when I've got my tongue buried deep inside of her is an impossible task, but I manage it somehow, only long enough to flip us around so I'm on my back again, this time with her big, round ass facing me as she straddles me on all fours.

Then her mouth is on the head of my aching cock, kissing it gently before I even have the chance to put my mouth back on her.

"Fuck, Scar," I moan, my hands reaching for her ass and squeezing it.

I spread her open for me enough to lick her pussy again.

My entire body shivers in pleasure as she licks along the length of my cock before swallowing me down completely. The warmth of her mouth almost has me coming down her throat immediately, liquid fire spreading through me from sheer pleasure. The fireplace seems to be getting hotter too, but it's not unpleasant at all.

Especially not when Scar cups my balls and squeezes them while swirling her tongue around the head of my cock.

"I'm going to come very quickly if you keep playing with my balls, wife," I warn, barely managing to move any muscle because pleasure has turned my limbs to putty.

"What if that's my goal?" she asks, squeezing my balls again as she sucks me down until her gag reflex sets in.

Desperation grabs hold of me, and I spread her pussy again to lick along the length of it. I thrust my tongue inside of her, tasting her, then move onto her clit because I know she loves it when I do that. Scar moans around my cock, never stopping her movements. She dials my pleasure higher and higher while I eat her out, bringing me even closer to my release.

The vibrations of her next moan, combined with her sucking on the head of my cock and kneading my balls has me coming so hard, the loudest groan escapes me as my legs start shaking. My cock is throbbing with its release, and Scar wastes no time sucking me down, drinking down every single drop of me.

Puñeta.

I slide my fingers inside of her, stroking her G-spot until she's screaming my name, following me straight over the edge. My thumb is still on her clit, even with my pleasure-clouded mind telling me to thrust into her mouth to elongate my orgasm for as long as possible.

What's more important to me is feeling her come around my fingers.

We stay in the same position for several moments, trying to catch our breaths and come back to reality. I take my time kissing her pussy, showing it some love after the not so gentle way I was eating her out and fucking her with my fingers. I kiss every single inch until she shakes a little, telling me that she's reaching her limit before she's getting too overstimulated.

I know Scar's body better than my own at this point, so I immediately ease away, turning her around and lying her down beside me. Running a hand through her hair, I place a soft kiss to her lips. My wife is having none of the carefulness, though. She kisses me as if she hasn't in years, her fingers slipping into my hair at the same moment her tongue enters my mouth. She tastes like me, and I'm convinced I taste like her, and both of us, being possessive of each other in ways we've never been of other people, are fucking loving it.

"Will you marry me again?" I say after a while of me absentmindedly running my fingers down her back while she does the same to my chest.

"We just got married, Julián," she reminds me with her sunshine smile, and I rub my nose over hers, completely unbothered.

"A year ago. Maybe we should get married yearly. Make it a tradition," I say and kiss the corner of her smile.

"I'll make you a deal, for every single one of your abs, we can get married. So, if I'm counting right..." She trails off as she brings her fingers to them. "One, two, three, four, five, six, seven, eight." She touches each ab as she counts aloud. "We can get married eight times in our lifetime."

I chuckle as soon as the words have left her, pushing against her back to bring her chest flush against mine.

"That sounds like a fair deal," I reply, kissing the other corner of her smile.

The fireplace is crackling behind us, the only sound breaking through the comfortable silence that surrounds us. I go back to trailing my fingers down her back.

Scar's head is lying on my bicep, her favorite pillow, while I smile down at her. Those blue eyes of hers are closed, enjoying my touch and the calm we somehow always manage to find when it's only the two of us.

I study her scar, the faint mark still as beautiful to me now as it was the day I met her.

"I'm going to miss being your race engineer," she says, opening her eyes to show me the sadness in them.

"I'm going to miss being able to go everywhere with you, but I'm too happy about you finally getting to live out your dream to be too upset about it," I say, which isn't a lie entirely. I'm so happy she gets to do what she's always dreamt of, but it would be a lie to say I'm not sad we'll be apart for so long.

We've spent the last four years working together in one way or another, the last two with her as my race engineer in smaller motorcycle racing categories—Moto3 and Moto2.

"Let's be honest, Julián, you're not as upset because I've made it up to you—" She trails her hand down my body and toward my very excited cock. "—several times." Scar wraps her hand around it, and it jumps to attention, making me hiss out a breath.

"There is nothing to make up for, but I'll take any excuse to get your hands on me." I lift my fingers to her throat, carefully wrapping them around it. Scar's eyes flutter the way they do when she's turned on, so I apply a small amount of pressure on either side, feeling her racing heart beneath my fingertips.

"Twenty-two races, husband. We will have twenty-two more races together."

She strokes my cock as she speaks, and as much as the topic of conversation saddens me, I'm thrusting into her hand, more pleasure coursing through me as if I hadn't had enough already.

Then again, there is no such thing as *enough* when it comes to Scarlette Alvarez.

"Twenty-two races to win the championship with Hawke," I say, but the moan that slips out of me after is entirely out of my control.

"You've done well during testing. You're fast, determined, and one of the best motorcycle racers I have ever seen. We will win and we will do it together," she says, rubbing her thumb over the head of my cock where precum is already leaking because of how hard I am.

"Compliment me again, love, and I'll fuck you hard enough so that both of us can't walk tomorrow."

A wicked smile covers her face as she closes the distance between our mouths.

"Your cock is so thick and hard, I can't wait to have it back inside me and come all over it again."

It takes no effort at all to roll her onto her back, spread her legs wide, and thrust back inside of her while she screams in pleasure.

Even if we lose, even if everything is lost in the world, as long as I have Scar in my life, I know everything will be fine.

She is my other half.

She is the best part of me.

She is my soul's matching piece.

No matter how dark the world gets, her colors will light it straight back up, and I will soak in her rainbow for as long as I'm allowed to breathe the same air as her.

My race engineer.

My wife.

Mi arcoíris.

Chapter 4

Scarlette

MotoGP Qualifying differs a lot from Formula One Qualifying. In F1, there are three tiers and the times set during practice don't play a role in the positions most of the time. Q1, Q2, and Q3 are also all different lengths of time.

MotoGP works differently.

There is only Q1 and Q2, and they are each fifteen minutes long. The top ten racers from the practice sessions get an immediate ticket into Q2, so to speak, and the two fastest racers from Q1, of the remaining twelve racers, also get from Q1 into the next tier.

There are twenty-two racers.

Eleven teams.

If I'm being honest, I had no idea what any of them were called before I met my husband. Now, I know them by heart.

Hawke CWM MotoGP.

Prima Pantera MotoGP Team.

Löwe Racing.

Fuoco MotoGP.

Phoenix Racing MotoGP Team.

Saturn Racing Team.

Zeitgeist Racing MotoGP Team.

Clover Racing.

Triangle Racing MotoGP Team.

Mariposa MotoGP.

Black Widow Racing.

Julián was one of the top ten racers during practice yesterday, so he's already in Q2. We're watching the others fight for their spot in Q2 while I look over some data with my husband.

"I think if we change the setup slightly here, we can maximize the performance of the bike even more." I point at the screen to let him know what I mean, and he nods several times as he processes the information.

"I trust you. Do whatever you think is best."

Julián gives me a single nod, and I smile at him before watching him walk toward his bike. I know it kills him not to be able to kiss me or hug me before he goes racing, but we've both agreed to keep things professional until after the races are done. Of course, I'll hug him and he'll kiss me when he wins a race, but not before, not during Qualifying. There is a time and place, and my husband and I are capable of keeping our hands off each other while we're at work.

However, I do take another few seconds to admire his perfect ass in those racing leathers of his, doing my best not to drool.

There is something about those leathers...

For one, they keep my Storm safe.

For two, all of my favorite parts of his spectacular body are highlighted.

Turning back to my screens, I ignore all those thoughts and focus entirely on every little task at hand. Being a race engineer means having a million responsibilities and things to do in very little time during race weekends.

Ten of the racers don't make it out of Q1, leaving the rest of the grid to head into Q2. Julián is completely dressed now, gloves on and helmet on his head, and I smile at the lavender and rainbow design he had incorporated to always have me with him on the bike. I'm not sure if it's for good luck or, I shiver even thinking about it, because he wants a piece of me to be there with him in case anything bad happens.

Either way, I'm with him, and I love that when the cameras focus on his helmet, they'll show the whole world the design he spent so long on.

The one he had made for me.

Julián's movements become ten times stiffer in all of his protective gear, and the sight of it calms some of my worries. I've watched him crash a dozen times by now, and he's always walked away with minimal injuries because of this very gear, so as uncomfortable as I know it is, it keeps him safe. Plus, I think he looks incredible in it, and every time he puts it on, he makes sure to leave his chest unzipped so I can zip it up for him. I'll never not get weak in the knees seeing him in that blue, red, and white suit with his trained chest and beautiful dark golden skin fully on display for me.

I shake my head, trying to refocus on the task at hand.

We're in Thailand for the first race of the season, and it's incredibly hot and humid. The setup of the bike is adjusted to the high temperatures of the track, and the tires we've chosen are also made to last.

Twelve riders make their way onto the track during Q2, setting competitive times. Hawke had been sponsoring Julián for years until Hawke CWM, the MotoGP division, finally offered him a spot in MotoGP.

Julián sets a stunning lap time that brings him into the number one spot in Q2. Sadly, it doesn't last long because when his teammate, Viktor Elonzo, crosses the finish line after his fast lap, he moves to the top. He takes the first place for now, and I study the screens in front of me, doing my best to figure out where Julián is losing the most time. If there is something in his setup I can change to help him. If there's something wrong with the bike that could potentially be slowing him down.

Everything on my end is working as it should be, so it's entirely up to Julián to maximize the speed of the bike on the track.

Unlike F1, there is no radio communication between race engineers and riders, which means the only way to communicate with Julián is through hand signals through the fence as he races by or using pit boards to present messages to him.

If I had the ability to speak to him, I'd be telling him to accelerate faster in corner three, hit the brakes later, and use the momentum to spiral him forward. All things he probably already knows or will figure out given some more time, so it may be for the best that there is no radio communication like there is in F1.

So, I keep my mouth shut, trusting he will send a lap time fast enough to take first place. It's as important as in F1 to qualify in a good place for the race the next day. The further up you are on the grid, the bigger your advantage.

I need him to have an advantage.

With the weight of his father's company's fate resting on his shoulders, if he doesn't do well in the first Qualifying, in the first race, the doubts are going to follow him for the rest of the season.

It's added pressure that I wouldn't be able to take away from him. Added pressure he'd be carrying for the next eight months. Added pressure that might destroy him before he has a chance to save the one thing he never thought he had to fight for.

There are three minutes left in Q2. Julián has dropped to P5, but he's going for another fast lap. My eyes glue themselves to my screens, watching all of the data and times as they come in throughout the lap. In corner three, Julián does exactly as I would have told him to, but as he exits the corner, yellow flags are waved in the second sector.

"No," I blurt out, watching Julián have to abort his fast lap.

He slows down.

One of the Black Widow Racing riders went too low in the corner and lost control of his bike, ultimately slipping off it. He crashes out of Q2, which is why the yellow flag is waved in the second sector.

There isn't enough time for any of the riders to set another lap time, so the places that they were in before the crash are the places they will be in for tomorrow's race.

Viktor is first.

The Prima Pantera racers are taking up places two and three.

One of the Phoenix riders is in fourth.

Julián is fifth.

The rest of the grid follows after, and even though it's not the worst position to start in, fifth is hardly ideal, especially for the first race of his MotoGP career in Hawke CWM, the team that has won five championships in a row.

Crap.

Julián is stress-baking.

I don't know when he went out to buy all of these ingredients after the Qualifying because he was with me almost the whole time, but I'm simply going to assume he had them delivered here so he could go straight to baking after his shower.

He's got a bit of flour smudged right beside where his birthmark sits on his cheek, and I can't help but smile at how adorable he looks. Stressed, yes, but also so cute with his eyebrows pulled together and his frown securely placed on his face.

"Baby, would you like to talk about it?" I ask because as much as I'm enjoying staring at his handsome face and naked torso, studying his muscles is not as important as getting him to talk to me.

It's a close thing, though.

"To be honest, *arcoíris*, there is nothing to talk about. I'm angry, upset, and nervous. Baking is one of two things that helps me get my frustrations out, so that's what I'm doing," he explains, stopping his movements long enough to look at me. Because he always looks at me when he speaks. He stops everything when I open my mouth.

"What's the other thing?" I ask simply to tease him.

"I'm more than happy to show you, but you have established a rule of no sex when you're on the first two days of your period," he replies, sending heat straight into my cheeks.

"That's for your own good. I bleed too much on the first two days," I remind him, but he shrugs.

"We've got condoms and a shower. I don't see the issue." Of course, he doesn't. My husband, being the man he is, doesn't find periods disgusting in the least.

It's one of the many reasons I love him so much.

He doesn't ever make me feel horrible about something as natural as having a period, and the thought of that alone always makes me fall harder for him.

"I could also still make you feel good with my mouth, but you don't want that either." He huffs and shakes his head.

"If I'm not allowed to make you come, you're not allowed to make me come." I can't help but grin at his frustrated expression.

"Then continue baking. I'll be here with my hot water bottle, watching you work," I say, placing my elbow on the table I'm sitting at before resting my cheek in the palm of my hand. A small smile curls the corners of his mouth as he takes me in while I ogle him, but he goes back to baking without another word.

His brown, wavy hair is still wet from the shower, and I study the droplets that fall down his bare torso before trailing my eyes up to his face. His differently colored eyes, his left one brown and the right one a mix of green and brown, show all of the emotions he's trying to keep off his face by frowning, but I see through him easily.

It's only when he finishes his third batch of chocolate chip cookies, one of my favorite things he bakes, that he opens his mouth again.

"I could have set a faster lap time. I could have been first. I could have—" He cuts himself off as he drops the tray he was using for the cookies on the stove.

He looks at me, and it's like he's calling my name, so I get up and move toward him. As soon as I'm in front of him, his hands move to my hips, and he pulls me against him, resting his forehead against mine.

"Could have, could have, could have," I say, and he grins with his eyes closed.

"Yeah," he replies, letting out a soft sigh.

"Doesn't get you anywhere," I remind him.

"I know, love, but I had to let it out."

"Then let it out. Let everything out because you will need a clear head for tomorrow," I say as I run my hands through his soft hair.

"You're my clear head." I chuckle in response, and he kisses my smile. "P5 sucks," Julián adds, rubbing his nose over mine as he shakes his head.

"It means nothing, my Storm. Nothing. What matters is how you finish. It's just one race, too. I know it's the first one, but if it goes to shit, you have an entire season to improve," I remind him, and he nods in agreement, kissing my lips again.

"You see. You're my clear head."

He squeezes my hips once before wrapping his arms around me and hugging me to his chest. Mine fly around his neck as he nuzzles his face into the crook of my neck, inhaling the lavender oil I applied there.

"We will win. If not tomorrow, then the next race. We will get that championship, Julián. I know we will."

Chapter 5

Julián

Race day.

I'm sweating in my gear, waiting on the grid for the warm-up lap.

From my practice sessions here on the Buriram International Circuit, I've realized I'm definitely not the strongest when it comes to taking corners. This track has a lot of sharp corners, and I have yet to find a balance between going too low and not going low enough. It's difficult to find a balance when racing motorcycles, especially because these aren't ordinary road bikes. They are manipulated and built in a way that abides by the rules of MotoGP while also maximizing speed.

This is a tough sport.

One wrong move, and your race is over. It takes patience, control, strength, and several other things I'm not entirely sure I excel at just yet. Not that I have much of a choice at the moment. It's either being the best or losing, and losing is definitely not an option.

Too much is on the line.

Starting fifth is shit, but I'll make the best out of this situation. Moaning and whining about it won't change anything.

Winning seems impossible from fifth place, but I've won from further back. Maybe not in MotoGP, but I've overtaken more than four riders in the past. With a good strategy, which I have thanks to Scar, there is nothing that can stop me.

Stop us.

I look down at my virtual pit board at my dashboard where Scar is going to send all of the important information I will need throughout the race. Anything from updates on our strategy or safety alerts, it all shows up on this pit board. They can also use physical ones that they hold out for me to read as I race by, but this supplementary system is quite useful.

The sighting lap seems like forever ago when we finally get to take our warm-up lap, all twenty-two of us steering from side to side in order to get heat into our tires. My nerves are going through the roof because this is my first race in MotoGP. I'm a rookie in this sport, a rookie on one of the fastest bikes, if not *the* fastest. I have a lot to prove to everyone watching. My teammate, Viktor, is starting from first position.

Fuck me.

It's so hot that sweat rolls down my forehead within seconds of the warm-up lap, and I'm already dreading how the rest of the race is going to go. I'm going to need an ice bath after this.

The crowd beside us roars as we race by, and I can't help but think of yesterday when Scar and I ran into some fans who were so excited to meet me. While MotoGP isn't nearly as popular as Formula One, there are still about a hundred and eight thousand people attending the Grand Prix today, and I'm grateful for each and every one of them that are holding up my number, fourteen, and my team's colors.

I've been popular in this sport since I started racing in Moto3. At first, it was very few people, but then I started winning races. I started proving myself, and everyone suddenly knew my name.

It also helped that they considered me a good guy off the track too, but that image was mostly created through a video of Scar and me dancing in the rain going viral. If it was up to me, my personal life would stay entirely personal. Everything I share with her would be kept off the internet, but at the same time, this way the entire world knows I belong to her, that she belongs to me, and I can hardly complain.

As a matter of fact, I smile everytime I think about being so publicly taken. I want to be taken in every way to make sure no one gets any ideas about my commitment to my wife.

The ring on my finger isn't enough to keep some people away, but I've still got a mouth, and I'm more than happy to tell them how taken I am.

As soon as we get back to the grid from our warm-up lap, my heart jumps into an even faster pace. In moments like these, I wish Scar was in my ear because there is nothing in the entire world that calms me as much as the sound of her voice. She's taught me a lot about mental health throughout our relationship. I knew about anxiety long before we met because of Elias, but every experience varies, and Scar teaches me about hers daily. Sometimes it's things we learn together. With my mental health, it is always things we learn together because I have no fucking clue what goes on in my head most days. But she's patient. Fuck, no one is as patient as her when it comes to mental health, or most things in life really.

I shake my head to force away every thought that doesn't belong in my mind during the race.

I have to concentrate.

Later, I can go back to thinking about Scar.

Once all the riders are lined up at their places on the grid, the lights ahead and on top of us turn on all at once. My hands grip the handlebars tighter, more sweat dripping down my back as I wait.

Another round of nerves washes through me, so I take a deep breath to settle myself. I center myself by squeezing even tighter.

Then, the lights disappear.

All of us dart ahead.

I overtake two riders within the first lap, but Viktor and Joseph from Prima Pantera are still ahead of me, battling for first while I try to chase them down.

There are twenty-six laps in the entire race.

I have twenty-four laps left to get them.

Adrenaline is pumping through my veins as I go after them. Every lean in the corner feels like a dangerous move, but I still go as low as possible while maximizing my speed to catch up to them.

I look to the side of the track to see the monitor with the time gap between us, groaning because they have already created a much bigger one than I would like. The heat is blaring down, my racing suit sticking to my skin. It's an entirely uncomfortable feeling that intensifies with every lap that passes.

There is no pitstop in MotoGP unless the track conditions change, so there is nothing stopping me from focusing entirely on chasing after Viktor and Joseph. Scar is the one in charge of my setup, and it feels absolutely perfect. My bike races across the track smoothly, and I see the time gap closing as I pass by the boards.

Joseph has backed off a little, simply staying close enough as to not wear out his tires too quickly. This sport is all about strategy. Viktor's strategy is obviously to push as hard as possible from the beginning to create a gap, but it's not that easy with Joseph sticking to him as if a rope was tied between their bikes, which is good for me because it means my teammate cannot get too far.

I can still get him.

The next ten laps are hell.

My body feels heavier in this heat.

I'm used to racing in all different types of weather conditions. It's even part of my training to get used to extreme heat and at the same time the cold as well, but today feels more brutal for some reason.

Maybe it's the added pressure. Maybe I'm not as prepared as I thought I'd be. Either way, there is no time to whine about it. I have about ten laps left to catch my teammate and the man chasing him.

It's a battle.

Once I catch up to them, they're both already in a rhythm of attacking and defending. But at least they weren't paying enough attention to me to see how quickly I've closed the gap between us, so I take their surprise as an advantage.

All three of us go into the next corner together, but I take it tighter than Joseph, allowing me to slip past him and into second place, but he's right there in the following corner and takes back his second place.

No, not his.

Mine.

I accelerate, going faster than my team would advise me to go as we head down the main straight, braking later than is advisable.

The momentum sends me forward, and I overtake Joseph again, this time making it stick.

There are five laps left.

My tires are degrading and slowing me down, but luckily, the same seems to be happening to Joseph because I create a gap between him and me.

At the same time, I'm getting closer to Viktor.

Laps pass, and we're finally fighting for first place.

I throw everything I have at him.

I give it my all.

And yet...

Viktor crosses the finish line ahead of me. He snatches the first win of the season, and a wave of defeat hits my system. My teammate does a wheelie in front of me, but I can't celebrate with him, no matter how great this is for our team. We're officially leading the Constructors' Championship, but all I can think about is the fact that I've lost the first race.

And if I've lost the first race, how will the rest of the season go?

I know it's fucking ridiculous to let these thoughts infiltrate. One race doesn't decide shit, but I'm vulnerable to these thoughts at the moment.

There is no stopping them.

We go for another lap before bringing our bikes to the first, second, and third place sign. I stay on it for another moment, my legs feeling weak from exhaustion and defeat. The only thing propelling me off my bike is the sight of Scar standing at the boundaries that surround us with a soft smile on her face. Her scar is even more visible today than normally, and I find it so beautiful that she doesn't hide it.

I move toward her, hating how tight this fucking racing suit is because it constricts my movements as I wrap my arms around Scar, allowing her comfort to seep into every part of me. She clings to me, her headphones knocking against my helmet, and I wish I'd have taken it off before hugging her so I could kiss her lips and let her wash away the rest of the world.

It would dull the disappointment, the ache in my chest.

"Good job, baby," she says, but she holds me tighter because she knows this isn't something I will celebrate.

She knows I'm not happy.

She knows *me*.

This thought alone settles all of the turmoil inside of me, and I sink further into her embrace, holding onto my rainbow for dear life because she's mine.

My entire life.

Chapter 6

Julián

Argentina was good to me.

It was only the second race of the season, but I came second again, this time with Viktor in fifth, which means I'm leading the championship for now. I didn't win, but at least I can stop beating myself up over not having won a race because I'm *leading*.

I'm in first place.

There were twelve days between the first and second race, and I was mentally destroying myself over the loss for all twelve of those days.

Scar did everything to cheer me up, but I think the grief of losing my father, the one I thought I'd worked through, is hitting me tenfold now that I'm on the brink of losing his legacy.

"My love, grief is not something you work through to the point where nothing triggers you anymore. Grief is a living thing inside of you that you can only learn to live with on your own terms. That doesn't mean you're not allowed to have bad days when it flares up. It doesn't even mean that you'll eventually stop feeling it as if it were nothing more than a suppressed thought," Scar said a few days ago, after I had a panic attack and couldn't get off the floor as I repeated "I thought I worked through this" about twenty times.

"Allow yourself to feel whatever you need to feel in any way makes you feel better afterward," she added, and I ended up simply looking up at her while she played with my hair, my head in her lap, wondering how the fuck I got so lucky to have the most wonderful person in the entire world by my side.

Wondering what I did to deserve living at the same time as her.

Wondering what I need to do to ensure she finds me and I find her in the next life too.

To celebrate a successful race weekend, Scar and I decided to go out with Leonard and Chiara Tick. We've been friends for a few years now, and they came to support me for the second Grand Prix.

Well, he and Chiara did as well as another friend.

Leonard hasn't had a sip of alcohol all night because he doesn't want to risk any being near Chiara, and the Italian woman has rolled her eyes several times already, mumbling that he should have a drink if he wants one, that their baby will be fine. Considering she's pregnant, she's wearing heels so high, I'd have broken an ankle just trying them on, but she's moving around effortlessly.

Not as effortlessly as Scar, though, who looks like a goddess I was born to worship.

She's wearing a skin-tight satin dress which is hugging her curves in a way that makes my mouth water. It hits her mid-thigh, and her stomach, legs, breasts, arms, all of her generous features are on display. She's in heels even higher than Chiara's, putting her almost at eye level with me.

I have a hard time looking away, so I don't try.

She's moving her hips from side to side, her arms lifted above her head before she slowly drops them, running her hands over her curves. My entire body heats with desire, but I stay glued to the table Leonard and I are standing at, giving our wives space as they enjoy themselves on the dance floor.

I notice Chiara squeezing Scar's arm before stepping toward us, holding her baby bump. She moves directly toward her husband, a small smile on her lips as she places her hands on his chest, trailing them up until they reach his neck.

With little effort, she drags his face down, her lips meeting his for a brief moment before she leaves him where he is, sliding a singular hand across his chest.

Leonard's eyes stay closed for several moments as he sways on his feet, and I can't help but chuckle because I get it.

I really do.

"Where did she go?" I ask when he finally looks at me again.

"Washroom, I believe. I'm not entirely sure. That woman kisses me, and everything vanishes. It's dangerous," he explains and runs a hand down his face, letting out a breathless laugh.

My attention shifts back to Scar, who is free and uninhibited as she continues dancing.

I'm about to go join her when someone stops me.

"Gentlemen," a very familiar voice says as he approaches us, too, and I drop my head in defeat as I shake it. "Have you missed me?"

"You were gone for two minutes, Adrian. You could have stayed away two hours, and the answer would still be 'no.'" Leonard's words are followed by an irritated frown that he throws Adrian's way.

But I know that's all an act.

Leonard Tick loves Adrian Romana like somebody loves a family member. He is very attached to the Monegasque, no matter how much he pretends not to be.

Me, on the other hand?

I find him awfully annoying.

Charming?

Sure.

How anyone could resist this man's charm is beyond me, but he's also a pain in the ass. An attractive pain in the ass that I wish I could keep away from Scar because he has that smile. A smile I know has made people fall at his feet. I love and trust my other half more than anything in the world, but I don't trust Adrian not to try and steal her away with *that smile*.

"What about you, Storm? Did you at least miss me a little?" he asks as he leans his elbows on the table and closes the distance between us.

"I know you have a crush on me, but a bit of personal space would be nice," I remind him, scowling in the way I tend to do when I'm not looking at Scar.

"Please, Storm, I don't have crushes on married men. That gets much too complicated." But the fucker winks at me and takes a sip of his water, never breaking eye contact with me.

I don't back down from this weird staring contest either.

Not until I notice a man walking toward the dance floor, determination in his face and in the confident way that he moves. A red flag goes off when my eyes follow his gaze to where Scar is currently rolling her hips, showing off her perfect ass. I see his hand reaching out long before he's near her, and I push off the table and close the distance between us.

I barely register Leonard and Adrian following because there is only one goal.

Prevent that guy from putting his hand on my wife.

My fingers snake around his wrist a second before he makes contact, and I pull it away, keeping the very inhuman sound, a warning and threat, to myself because I'm not an animal. Even if I'd like to tear his head off for even attempting to touch Scar without her consent.

Therapy has been helping her feel comfortable to go out and be around people, even having strangers touch her, but he was going right for her lower back, maybe even for her ass, and that would have triggered her anxiety.

On top of that, I'm simply a very possessive man, and I hate seeing anyone putting their hands on her in a flirty way.

"If you want to keep the hand attached to your body, I suggest keeping it off women who didn't give you permission to touch them," I warn, releasing him and stepping in front of Scar when she turns around. It's my way of shielding her, but her fingers lace through mine, telling me she's right here.

"Relax, man. I didn't mean any harm," the guy responds with an American accent, clearly unbothered by my threat.

"Oh, so if I punch you in the throat and knee you in the balls, but claim I didn't mean any harm, then it's fine?" Adrian challenges, towering over the guy by at least two heads. He's smiling, which makes him appear more frightening than charming at the moment, and the way he's defending Scar, defending me, is the first time that I get it.

Adrian has always been this flirty, nothing ever gets to him, unserious guy around me. He's the very opposite right now. He's like a protective mountain, ready to tear a person limb from limb for… us.

"You want to take this outside, asshole?" the short man asks, and I want to respond, to tell him we won't be doing that, but I'm too fascinated by Adrian to do so.

"So you can get your ass handed to you by a millionaire F1 driver? Do you truly want that plastered everywhere in the news?" Adrian challenges, crossing his arms in front of his chest to appear more unbothered than he is.

I never thought he would ever be violent. He doesn't strike me as the type of person to resort to that, but I'm not so sure anymore.

The man takes a step toward Adrian, but right as he attempts to grab him by the collar, his hands drop again and he cries out in pain.

"Touch Adrian, and I will break my promise to my husband that I won't fight anyone while pregnant," Chiara says, making me stand a little straighter as I take in the image of her pulling on the guy's ear and yanking it down enough to bring him pain.

"Who the fuck are you?" he cries out, and I notice the smallest hint of a smile on Chiara's lips.

"I'm a woman who'd put a man in the hospital for her family, no matter the consequences, so I'd reconsider if harassing someone is really worth the damage I'll do to your face." She releases him, and Leonard is right beside her then, attempting to pull her behind him, but the Italian woman isn't having it.

"I was just trying to have some fun. What the fuck is wrong with you all?" he asks as he walks away, rubbing his ear as he does.

"Why do sleazy men always have to try and ruin a woman's fun night out?" Chiara asks as she looks at Scar, her frown turning into a soft expression. "Are you okay, *bella*?"

"I'm fine. Truly," she says, and I squeeze her hand before turning to her and guiding her into my arms. Scar looks unbothered as she flings her arms around my neck, but I'm still stiff from anger. "Julián, baby, it's okay. Nothing happened," she assures me. "Let's celebrate this weekend and forget about what just happened." She kisses my jaw and runs her fingers through my hair.

"I can't forget it. I think this was the first moment I've started to like Adrian Romana," I admit, and he must have been close enough to hear even with the music blaring, because his head shoots my way before a bright smile covers his face.

"I knew I'd break through your walls! I knew it!" he announces and skips toward me, wrapping his arms around Scar and me. "This is the best moment of my life," he says as he suffocates us with his hug and love, and as irritated as I wish I could be, I notice Scar's bright smile, her sign of happiness.

I can't be mad at someone who brings out that smile.

"If I'd known violence turned you on, I'd have threatened to kick someone's ass long ago," Adrian says, making Scarlette burst into laughter.

"You had to ruin the moment, didn't you?" I ask him, still trapped in his embrace.

"Couldn't help it."

He gives us one last squeeze before releasing us, grinning like he's never been happier. None of us speaks again, but there is a strange sort of understanding weighing between us. He nods, and I nod, and then Adrian turns to Chiara, wrapping her in a bear hug. Leonard places a hand on his back.

Adrian means a lot to them. He loves them with his whole heart. They're a family in their own way, and a strange sort of longing shoots through my chest at the sight of it.

"I know you have this habit of not letting people in, but they are very good people. We can allow them to become more than occasional friends. We can let them become family, too." Scar's fingers slip to my cheeks, holding me close while we sway to the music.

"More family means more people to lose," I mumble, trying to look away, but her hold on me is strong enough to keep me in place.

Images of Jamie and my father flood my mind, and I hardly have the strength to push them away without a mountain of sadness crushing me.

"More family also means more people to love," she adds, and I feel my heart stutter.

"*Tiene sentido, mi arcoíris*," I reply, resting my forehead against hers.

"*Siempre tengo sentido, mi amo*r," she says, and I smile brightly, inhaling her lavender scent to let it calm me.

We continue to sway to the music, right until it picks up pace, and Scar urges me to dance properly with her. Since there is no resisting her, I join in, moving my hips in perfect harmony with hers.

"I'll try harder to let them in," I promise.

"Good, because I'm very fond of Chiara, and I'd love to spend more time with her," Scar says, and she should have really led with that because she knows I'd do anything for her happiness.

I'll befriend whoever she tells me to.

"I don't ever want to get on that woman's bad side," I mumble, making her giggle.

"Me neither," she replies and keeps giggling, sending my heart into palpitations.

"Are you sure you're okay?" I ask once she stops laughing, needing her vocal reassurance.

"I'm so okay. As a matter of fact, I'm happy. We're here with our friends, you're leading the championship. Life is very good at the moment, and I'm going to soak in this feeling for as long as the universe grants it."

I kiss her as soon as I'm sure she's finished speaking.

I kiss her because, deep down, I'm also happy.

I kiss her because it feels like a waste to spend a second without her mouth on mine.

CHAPTER 7

Scarlette

We're on the third race of the season here at the Circuit of the Americas. Because this track isn't too far from Moonville, Violet and Elias have decided to join us. Halo is also here, and he has yet to leave my side for even a second. I know he misses me as much as I miss him when we're apart, that's what happens when you become close friends for the duration of your university life, and I enjoy his proximity a lot.

Over my years of friendship with Halo, I've learned a lot about him. He's a driven, intelligent, and kind person who loves his family with his whole heart, but it took him a while to open up to me about his story.

Halo is pansexual. Relationships are unappealing to him because he's so busy taking care of his family, he doesn't think he could give a partner the attention they deserve, especially because his sister needs someone to go with her to all her races. That's another thing he only shared with me two years ago. His sister, Nachelle, is a racecar driver, and she's working her way up into F1. At least that's her dream, and I'm planning on asking Valentina for any tips she might have for the fifteen-year-old.

A year ago, he finally opened up to me about his dream of working in Formula One, too. He wants to become a technical director. It's a tough job to work your way up to, but Halo is so smart and he's so passionate about F1, I know he can do it. It's only a matter of time until someone discovers his potential and gives him the chance I know he deserves.

He also shared that he's half-American and half-Dominican, but he feels like he's lost his roots to his Mom's side of the family. He's told me that he often doesn't feel like he has a right to belong to that part of his family, his identity, because of his name and the way he looks. People have questioned his Dominican side because of these two things, which is why he didn't tell me until almost a year into our friendship. I think he's scared people will doubt him, question him because he doesn't fit this image they have created of what people from the Dominican Republic look like.

Halo is tall with brown hair, tanned skin, and icy-blue eyes. Although his Spanish is flawless, he's told me he feels insecure about the slight American accent that slips out at times when he doesn't concentrate. As a non-native Spanish speaker who's become mostly fluent through her husband's determination as a teacher, I don't hear it, but I know he does. He hears it because he's spent his life having people tell him he's not "Dominican" enough.

"What are you thinking about?" Vi asks as she steps next to me, hooking her arm through mine.

"Halo," I admit, and as if he heard his name from across the garage, his head snaps up and he looks our way.

"I get it. He *is* gorgeous," my best friend replies, and I burst into laughter.

"No, I wasn't thinking about him like *that*." I don't see anyone but my Storm that way.

"Like what?" Halo asks, smirking like he has no care in the world.

"None of your business, nosey," Violet replies and nudges him in the side. He doesn't waste a second throwing his arm around her shoulders, pulling her against his side.

"You don't have to tell me. I already know. But I have to put a stop to it, beautiful. I do not sleep with married people."

I give him the unimpressed look that statement deserves.

"Does it ever get exhausting carrying the weight of your humongous ego on your back?" I ask, but Halo furrows his brows, his look of disbelief answer enough for me.

"You should be nice to me. I drove all the way out here to see your husband win his first Grand Prix in MotoGP," Halo replies and squeezes Vi one more time before dropping his arm and making his way to my screens. He studies the data there, clearly lost in it now.

"How's Liliana? How are you feeling about being apart from her for the first time?" I ask as Violet reaches for her phone for the seventeenth time in twenty minutes.

"Slowly dying. It feels like there is a string between us and I have stretched it to the maximum, so any minute, I'm bound to recoil violently."

I smile comfortingly at her, the metaphor equally frightening to me as it is sweet. Frightening because I don't want children, so the thought of feeling this way as a mother scares me. Sweet because it's beautiful how much Violet loves her daughter. I hope one day, when I'm settled into my new job as Val's race engineer, after I end the season winning the championship with my husband, we'll be ready to get a pet. I've always wanted to have a dog. And cats. Maybe a fish tank. An axolotl perhaps, because they're *so cute*.

All I have to do is tell Julián I want these things and he will give me everything, but we also have to be prepared for the responsibility.

First, we have to make sure we don't lose everything he's built.

"You know you can go home at any point, Vi." She takes my hand in hers and squeezes as a smile lifts the corners of mouth.

"I know, but I want to be here. Watching Storm race is one of my favorite things," she replies, turning to the monitors as well.

Right at that moment, my husband walks into the garage, making my mouth water almost instantly. He's wearing his racing gear and that frown that always disappears as soon as he looks at me, which is probably why he doesn't right now. My husband is annoyed, and worry washes through my chest at the sight of him.

"Julián, what's wrong?" I ask as I approach him.

Qualifying starts in less than thirty minutes, and there is still a lot to do to prepare for it, but he doesn't seem to care as he takes my hand in his and leads me out of the garage. We keep walking until we find an empty room with several tires in it and various other tools the mechanics use to work on the bike.

Julián shuts the door behind him, leaning against it once it's closed. I study him, the stiff way he moves from his irritation and the racing gear. His two differently-colored eyes are on me as he takes one deep breath, probably to slow his racing mind or heart. I'm not entirely sure which it is as he crosses the room, closing the distance between us.

"Viktor and I got into a fight. He approached me, telling me that the team should prioritize him this season, and when I told him to go fuck himself, he started yelling at me. Telling me I'm worthless as a teammate. That I'm not as worthy of the title as he is because he has been in this sport for much longer. That I'm a talentless piece of shit."

Anger like I've never felt before consumes every little part of me.

"MotoGP teams don't freaking prioritize riders over each other. This is not Formula One. There is no number one and number two rider. Who does he think he is this— this—" I cut off, trying to restrain myself from saying some very rude things about Viktor, things I've never said about a person in my life.

"You can use vulgar language when it comes to him, *arcoíris*. If anyone deserves it, he does," Julián assures me, and the little smile that tilts up the right side of his mouth has some of the anger lifting off my chest.

Some.

Not all.

"Yes, I can insult him. I can waste my breath on cursing him out, but I'd rather spend it telling you how amazing you are. Viktor is nothing compared to you, husband. You are worthy of the championship. Of your spot in MotoGP. Of everything you dream to accomplish."

His gaze softens, and he finally lifts his hands to my cheeks, cupping them gently in his big hands. The hardness of his wedding band is a comfortable sensation against my skin, and I lean into his left hand to feel it even more.

"You're right. That is a much better way to use words," he says and leans down to press a gentle kiss to my lips.

"Yeah, but also, fuck that guy. He can eat a bag of dog shit."

My husband's laugh fills the room, and I grin in response, content with myself for finding a way to cheer him up. Even if it's only momentarily.

Once he's done laughing, he brings his mouth back to mine. We lose each other in the kiss for far too long, but it's hard to stop when Julián's hands trail all over my body, caressing every single curve he can touch.

"Go. We can finish this later," I say after managing to step back, both of us out of breath.

"*O puedo hacer venirte ahora*," he suggests, making me grin even more brightly at him as desire pools low in my stomach.

"Go get pole position." It takes every bit of self-control to get the words out, but it's important that he focuses now.

He groans in complaint, his hands squeezing my hips one last time as he kisses me again too, then steps away.

"Fine. I'll go kick his ass, snatch pole, then we get back to this."

One last kiss, and he grabs my hand, guiding me back outside so we can do our jobs.

And yes, kick Viktor's butt.

Watching Julián crash will never not stop my heart for a beat. My anxiety has a nasty habit of setting in a split second later until I'm breathing heavily, my hands are shaking, and sweat starts rolling down my back.

It only eases once he stops sliding and gets back up on his feet, but it takes him longer this time. His bike, having slammed into the barriers, is completely wrecked, so there is no way he will be able to continue in this race.

He's out.

Crap.

I shove my headphones off my head, dropping my face into my hands. Someone rubs my back comfortingly, and I tilt my head to see Halo staring at the screens with shock in his bright eyes.

"Is he going to be okay?" he asks, his attention trained on the monitors.

"The gear protects him. Don't worry," I assure both of us in the same breath.

His shoulders fall in relief, and mine do the same as Julián stands up and makes his way to the barriers where one of the marshals is already waiting for him. His head hangs low in defeat, and I know this is going to destroy the confidence he just built. If Viktor finishes 11th or higher, he's going to overtake my husband in the championship standings.

The Prima Pantera racers could overtake him, too. He could drop significantly in the standings all because of this single DNF.

And then he does.

Ten laps later, as the race comes to an end with Viktor winning the race, both Prima Pantera's occupying the next two positions, my husband drops all the way into fourth in the championship standings.

The tears of frustration that fall from his eyes in private, when I have my arms wrapped around him, have some dropping from my own eyes.

It's pointless to tell him this is only the third race. It's pointless to say a lot of things that are on my mind, so I simply hold him.

Tell him that I love him.

Assure myself he's okay by touching every part of his body.

CHAPTER 8

Julián

Qatar wasn't a great Grand Prix for me, but it wasn't the worst one of the season either. I came in third while Viktor came in sixth, which helped close the gap between us a little. The Prima Pantera drivers were struggling all weekend, which means they didn't come in first and second either. No. They were eleventh and sixteenth, sending me straight back into second place in the standings.

It's not first place, but it's better than nothing.

I've been doing my best not to let the result influence my emotions so much because I know it tears down Scar at the same time, and her mental health is more important to me than any title or company in the world.

But it's difficult. It's really difficult. I'm having a hard time distinguishing between losing a singular race and losing my father's company. It's not the same thing at all, rationally I know that, but distinguishing them isn't happening easily in my brain.

"Storm, *¿estás escuchando*?" Elias asks, his tone revealing how worried he is. I look at him on the screen of my laptop.

"*Entiendo todo*," I reply before leaning back in my seat and tapping my pen against the notepad on the desk they have here at the hotel in Spain.

We flew here for the fifth race of the season a few days ago, and since there was an entire week of no racing between Qatar and Spain, Scar and I decided to do some sightseeing here.

"*¿Entiendes todo o escuchaste todo?*" my best friend challenges, and I do my best not to roll my eyes.

"*¿Cual es la differencia?*" He shakes his head, then runs a hand over his tired face.

"Okay, I can tell you're done talking about this today, so I'll let you go. You probably have plans with your wife," he says right as Liliana starts screaming, the sound blaring through the monitor he has sitting beside him on the desk. "And I have a diaper to change," he adds with a little laugh. "We can pick this up tomorrow. The company's problems will still be there then."

"Unfortunately," I mumble, bringing a smile to his face.

"Yeah. Unfortunately."

He leaves the meeting, and I turn to the paperwork on my desk, scanning the pages for the millionth time.

The bank is lenient enough to give us time until the end of my season, but I'm also trying to find ways to make some money to relieve a bit of the pressure of whether I win the championship or not.

"Julián."

My head snaps up instantly at the tone of her voice.

Over the years, I have studied every single lilt and intonation of my wife's voice. I know when she wants to fuck because it drops an octave. I know when she's happy because it sounds higher than normal. I know when she needs her space because it's more monotone.

When she's anxious?

Her voice shakes.

I jump out of my seat and cross the room to get to where she's standing in the doorframe. Her hands are trembling and her breathing is shallow, uneven. Her eyes have that faraway look in them that always breaks my heart a little, and her lips and face have become unnaturally pale. I know she's trying to get at least her breathing back under control because she inhales deeply, but it's useless. Once she spirals into her anxiety attack fully, there is no magical stop button to get her out. The only way to get out is to go through, and I made her a promise long ago that I'd always do my best to get to her so she doesn't have to be alone when it happens.

She can be. I know that. Scar is the strongest person I have ever met, but this is about her having to be alone when she's anxious, and she doesn't.

Not if I'm right here or I can get to her quickly.

"Okay, love, let's sit down. Alright?" I ask her, grabbing her forearms to stabilize her, show her I'm right here because I know her eyes are unfocused.

Scar nods several times until eventually, her head continues the motion, shaking in rhythm with her hands. Her mouth is slowly starting to cramp up, her lips forming a slight O-shape because she no longer has control over her facial muscles.

I guide her to our bedroom in this hotel suite, gently lifting her onto the mattress before pushing her back by her shoulders so she leans into the pillows.

"I'll be right back," I promise her, rushing out of the room to grab some water, ice, her lavender, and all of the other things she takes in these situations to help her.

We have a routine now. It's happened often enough that I know exactly what she needs. Scar has become comfortable enough to allow her anxiety attack to take over with me present. She trusts me to bring her what she needs, to take care of her. Her attacks don't happen as often anymore as they did when we first started fake dating, but they are still very much a part of her life. Nowadays, they usually only happen when something triggers her, or when she gets scared or worried.

"Here you go, *mi arcoíris*," I say and bring the lavender oil to her wrists, carefully massaging it into her skin.

Then, I do the same to her temples and behind her ears.

She's still shaking, trembling through her anxiety attack. Sounds of pain and panic leave her as she clings to the plushy I bought her a while ago so she has something to hold onto during her anxiety attacks. It's in the shape of me, merch that a fan makes in my honor for other fans, or in my case, for me.

"Open your mouth," I say next, but she shakes her head to tell me she can't. "It's okay. I'll open it for you. Yeah?" She nods this time, so I bring my hand to her jaw, pulling on her chin to open her mouth wider. I put her drops, the ones she takes to help calm her, in her mouth. It's still cramping, so I help her tilt her head back to make sure she can easily swallow the drops. "Good?" I ask once I'm done, but Scar is falling deeper into her attack with every second.

So, I hold her. She clings to me, and I hold her close so she knows I'm not going anywhere. Tears are streaming down her cheeks too quickly for me to wipe them away, but I try my best.

"Let me know whenever you're ready for the ice cubes," I say after a few minutes of silence, with her still trembling in my arms and fighting to find her way back to reality.

"I'm ready," she says, her voice still shaking.

I reach for one of the cubes and place it against her lips, letting the coolness shock her system. It's supposed to help stop anxiety attacks, but Scar has found that it doesn't exactly stop it as much as it helps her focus on something other than her panic. She takes the cube into her mouth and sucks on it while I watch her trembling slow with every passing minute.

Eventually, she looks up at me, her eyes puffy and red from the crying. Exhaustion has covered her features, and it breaks my heart when more tears fall down her reddened cheeks.

"I hate those so much," she cries, her fingers gripping the front of my shirt harder.

"I know, my love." I kiss the top of her head, my fingers tightening around her arm. "Do you know what triggered this one?"

"I don't want to say," she mumbles so immediately, it's as if she was expecting my question and had that answer ready.

"You don't have to, but you know it'll make you feel better," I remind her, slowly stroking her dark hair. Her blue eyes avoid my gaze, but if I could see them, I know they'd tell me everything.

"I can't," she whispers, burying her face into my chest.

"Yes, you can."

"You'll hate yourself if I do. I know you."

Fuck.

"I did something?" The defeat in my voice is palpable, and she hears it too because Scar sits up immediately, her eyes finally meeting mine.

"No. You did nothing. Julián, you are as close to perfect as is humanly possible. One of your few flaws, however, is thinking everything is your fault when it isn't. So, I can't tell you. Not this time."

It kills me a little that whatever is bothering her, had her spiral into an anxiety attack, is something she isn't comfortable sharing because of *me*. Because of my inability to blame someone else for whatever is going wrong in our lives. I want her to always be able to share her worries and fears with me.

If I'm not her safe space, I'm doing something very wrong.

"I promise that whatever you tell me, I will not blame myself." Scar furrows her brows in disbelief, then narrows her eyes.

"Swear it on my life."

"I swear it on your life," I reply because there is no way I can break a promise as precious as her life.

"I spiraled into my anxiety attack because I went down the rabbit hole of what would happen if we lost the championship this season. What would happen to you.

Your dad's company. To Elias' guilt and mental state. There's so much pressure on both of us, and I couldn't stop the panic as it clawed itself into my chest."

Scar's gaze drifts to her hand where it rests on the bed, right next to mine, and I slide my fingers around hers to squeeze them comfortingly. We've discussed all the pressure that is resting on my shoulders. We've discussed what making mistakes on my part would mean, but we didn't get into how much pressure rests on Scar's shoulder to constantly perform at the highest level at her job. Because she blames herself too if our strategy doesn't work out during a race. We didn't discuss how this is affecting her mentally.

I made a promise to her not to blame myself, so I can't do that. Even if it's my father's company we're trying to save. Even if she's my race engineer and whenever I fuck up, I fuck it up for both of us. Even if there are countless more reasons for why this is all my fault.

This is not about guilt-tripping me. Scar would never want that, which is why she made me promise not to turn this on me.

"I wish I could take the pressure off you," I say instead of what I'd said if she hadn't made me promise.

Scar's expression softens.

"And I wish I could take it off you, but we can't. We will have to find better ways to deal with it," she says, crawling into my lap and placing her hands on each side of my neck.

"I can't think when you're touching me, wife. You know that," I mutter, fighting back the desire to kiss her and forget about the rest of the world at the same time.

"You don't have to think. There is nothing more we need to discuss. Sometimes, things have to be the way they are. We'll have to fight through this for the rest of the season, but we can do it. We can carry the weight of the pressure because it's us, you know? We can do anything together," she says and leans forward to hug me.

My tensed muscles relax at the contact, and I wrap my arms around her, kissing her temple.

"You're right. Things are what they are. We will get through this shitty phase and we will come out on top. But I'm begging you, Scar, when you feel yourself spiraling about these things, talk to me. Bottling them up is a recipe for disaster."

Scar lets out a little chuckle.

"I used to think we were a recipe for disaster," she admits, and I let out a deep laugh, feeling the usual ease I experience around Scar settle inside of me. "I didn't want to say anything because this isn't on my shoulders. It's on yours, and I have no right to feel so overwhelmed. It's your life, not—" No matter how much I despise cutting her off, I have to. She's spiraling down into some place I never, ever want her to go.

"Tú *eres mi vida*," I say. "*You*. Not the pressure of losing my father's company. Not my career. Not anything other than *you*. You are what is most important to me. I'm sorry life is so difficult at the moment. I'm sorry you have to carry this with me, but I want you to know you have every right to feel what you're feeling. Because you're my race engineer. You're my wife." I lift my hand to her neck to guide her toward me. "You have every right. Every. Right."

More tears fall down her cheeks at my reassurance, and I hug her to my chest, letting her cry against me. Guilt fills me to the brim before overflowing and dripping down my cheeks in response.

This is what marriage is all about. Sharing each other's heaviness so it feels a bit lighter. I don't want Scar to crumble under my responsibilities, but it would be a lie to say I don't breathe a little easier knowing we're in this together.

And yet...

"Say the word, and I'll find a way to take this onto myself entirely. I'll do whatever you need me to do. I promise." Scar shakes her head almost immediately.

"No, baby. I want to be in this with you. I just needed to let it out, and my anxiety forced it to come out this way."

She leans back, kissing my lips and crawling onto my lap to get closer. I shiver the second her breath ghosts mine, pure bliss replacing any other feeling inside of me.

"Thank you for helping me through it and keeping your promise not to blame yourself." She kisses me again, and as much as I want to respond, words evaporate as her tongue slips into my mouth.

The world evaporates.

Chapter 9

Julián

We're in England for the seventh race of the season.

Viktor is standing beside me on the trailer as we go around the track for the Rider Fan Parade. We haven't really spoken in weeks, since we had our fight, and I'm not planning on approaching him to fix our relationship. For all I care, he can be my enemy. I don't give a fuck if our team frowns at us for not getting along. I played nice. I respected his space. And then I was rewarded with an attack on my ability as a racer, my worth as one.

There is no forgiving that.

I wave at our fans, gritting my teeth every time I see a poster of Viktor blocking a poster someone made for me. It makes me wonder if people would be rooting for him if they knew what kind of a prick he is.

"Something bothering you?" he asks with a smug smile, throwing the look my way because he knows it pisses me off.

"Your presence. Care to remove yourself to make me feel better?" Viktor chuckles, entirely unbothered by my angry tone.

"No, I think I'll stay right here, mess with your mindset before the race," he replies, and I don't want to give him the satisfaction of walking away first, so I stay cemented in my spot.

"Hey, fuck face. Storm may have a problem chucking you off this damn trailer, but I sure as shit don't. Remove yourself before I remove you."

My head snaps in the direction of where the voice is coming from, curiosity filling me to the brim.

There he stands, one of the Fuoco MotoGP racers, with his hands on his hips, a disgusted look on his face, and impatience written into every fiber of his being.

"You're an aggressive one, aren't you?" Viktor asks, and I'm having the time of my life watching someone else deal with my stupid, arrogant teammate.

"Not aggressive, just sick and tired of bullies. We're grown men, not teenagers in high school. Stop acting like an insecure child and go fuck off. " Tanner Carrigan is tall and muscular, and intimidating. At least until Viktor leaves. Tanner's frown is replaced by a smile that he directs fully my way. "Sorry about that. I can't deal with assholes anymore."

The crowd takes that moment to cheer for us, and we turn to wave at them. Once we're around the corner, I face Tanner again.

"I don't recall ever having a conversation with you before. Why would you step in and defend me like that?" I ask, narrowing my eyes a little because I don't trust his intentions yet. Not when I don't know what they are.

"You're a newbie. You haven't had to deal with Viktor before, and I wanted to be nice. Has no one been nice to you in this sport yet?" he asks, genuinely shocked. His brown eyes study me like he doesn't quite believe me.

"Not so far, no. Isn't that normal?" I ask, standing to cross my arms in front of my chest to stop the ache inside of me.

"No, Storm, that's not normal." I furrow my brows, fighting back half a smile.

"How the fuck do you know that name?" I go by Julián in the MotoGP world. It makes it easier. Plus, it feels like the kind of name I only want my friends and the people in the small town I grew up in to use.

"I did my research on you, man. As soon as I heard you were joining the grid on the most competitive bike, I had to look into you. Into your successes and failures."

"That's a bit creepy, don't you think?" Tanner laughs at that.

"No, it's strategic. You have to know who your competition is. Plus, it's never a bad thing to find something from a person's past to potentially use against them. Like Viktor. Did you know that during one race weekend, he shit his pants during Qualifying and couldn't set times after that?" he asks and waves at more fans.

"You're kidding."

"Nope. That actually happened. So, next time he fucks with you, use that. He hates being reminded of it." Tanner nudges my shoulder with his before positioning himself beside me so we're both looking out at the crowd.

"You're evil for telling me that," I say to him, not stopping the small smile that is trying to cover my face.

"No, I'm your friend now, and friends look out for each other." I almost snort, but we're having a... tolerable conversation, so I don't ruin the moment.

"Thanks."

He nudges me again, and I smile even more. I don't direct it his way. I direct it at my fans, who are probably as surprised at my expression as I am to be giving it to them.

The rest of the parade is uneventful. Tanner keeps talking to me, and I listen closely, asking questions if I'm interested in what he's saying. He doesn't mind simply talking though, which means he goes on and on, even if I stay silent. He's a nice guy. Chatty, sure, but I also appreciate him trying to help me with my Viktor situation.

In a way, he's the first person in MotoGP who's trying to look out for me, the rookie, and my chest tightens uncomfortably at the thought.

So much so that after the parade, I make my way straight to Scar and hug her until the feeling subsides.

"Are you okay?" she asks, hugging me back, and her lavender scent combined with just *her* has my back untensing.

"*Te quiero mucho, arcoíris.*" I lean back to kiss her lips, and she melts against me, her bottled-up sunshine smile coming out. I kiss it, kiss her scar, then step back because I know she wants us to keep it professional here. She doesn't want to be called "Julián Alvarez's wife." No matter how good that sounds to me, here, at our place of work, I understand she wants to be Scarlette Alvarez.

Roots-Alvarez.

Whatever.

She insists I remember that she hyphenated her name. I insist that I could also simply go around telling people that she's mine and I'm hers. She didn't argue with me anymore, only giggled to herself because no matter what, she loves me more than anything.

"Want to know a secret?" she asks, stepping toward me and reaching up to place her hands on my neck. A smile covers my entire face because she's seeking out touching me right now, and it's the most wonderful thing in the world to me.

"Well, are you keeping secrets from me?" I tease, making her chuckle. My hands slip onto her hips, squeezing them and enjoying the way my hands are entirely full of her.

"I've only been keeping it for a few days, but I think it'll make you happy." I cock a brow, my curiosity piqued. "I don't know what it is, but I have a feeling today will be the day you get your first win. I didn't feel this way about any of the other races, this deep-rooted, gut feeling."

My hands squeeze her hips again, this time of their own volition. It should pressure me that she feels this way, but it has an oddly opposite effect. Her confidence fuels mine. I'm starting from pole. The weather is supposed to stay the way it is, sunny and free of rain. Viktor is in thirteenth because of issues he had with his bike during Qualifying. Everything is on my side today.

"Today?" I ask, my heart racing at the possibility of finally winning my first race.

"Today."

***

There are twenty laps in the British Grand Prix. The Silverstone Circuit is dry and during the sighting lap, I got to reacquaint myself with it today. There are no surprises, nothing at all that may prevent me from winning.

Except myself.

All my doubts I couldn't hear when I was with Scar earlier bombard my thoughts until they are all I hear.

For someone who has fought their way into MotoGP, shedding tears, blood, and sweat on his way to get to where I am, my confidence sure as fuck crumbles quickly.

Luckily, we're signaled to start the warm-up lap before I spiral down my dark thoughts.

My breathing is slightly uneven. With so much on the line, I have to be at the top of my game. There is no room for error. It's either I have the mindset to win, or I'll lose *again*. And that's not an option. Not with my wife sitting at her screens, counting on me to have what it takes to reach our dream.

Because it isn't just my dream anymore. It's ours. It's something we are working toward together.

Something we can only reach as a team.

The warm-up lap is uneventful, all twenty-two of us simply trying to get some grip into both tires. My heart has adapted this strange, uneven rhythm that makes it pound hard and completely out of its normal beat at the same time. It reminds me of how it used to be when I was around Scar. A combination of being nervous and anticipating the interaction. A feeling that reminds me that I'm alive. A feeling

I never knew what to do with until she showed me to chase it because there is hardly a better sensation than sensing the life coursing through your veins.

All of us line up on our spots on the grid when we get back from our warm-up lap.

The uneven rhythm in my chest continues, but I embrace it. I let confidence take hold of every part of me. I earned this spot in MotoGP. I won the championship in Moto2 and Moto3 with my beautiful wife on my team.

Today is my day.

And I won't let anyone take it from me.

Chapter 10

Scarlette

My breath always seems to get stuck in my throat right as all the lights appear above my husband. My eyes skip between where my data is displayed on a system to the footage of the entire grid waiting for the lights to disappear.

Then they finally do.

Julián shoots forward, ahead of the rest of the grid to keep his first place. The Prima Pantera racers are close behind, chasing him. My attention skips back to the data, the headphones on my ears tight in place to protect them from the surrounding sounds and also allowing me to communicate with other members of the team.

Twenty laps.

He only has to fight off those two fast panthers behind him for twenty laps.

I adjust Julián's setting a little as the laps roll on, optimizing them so his engine and aerodynamics are taking him as fast as possible. It's my responsibility to ensure that my rider can get the most out of his bike by adjusting the settings according to the data on my screens and his performance. The track conditions and how quickly the tires degrade naturally plays a big role as well.

My anxiety is a heavy rock that sits in my stomach, making me nauseous. It has a habit of staying with me even during races, but luckily, I'm usually too busy in my mind to take too much notice of it, which means it never pushes me into an anxiety attack. It's simply there, like the ring resting on my finger. I can feel the weight of it, can feel its presence, but it's something I've become so accustomed to that I don't exactly mind the weight of it.

Julián doesn't get a chance to breathe in the first five laps.

Joseph and Kwan, the Prima Panteras, are stuck to him like glue. When he goes into a corner, they follow him. When he wheelies to get more speed, so do they. They react to Julián, too. If he goes a little too wide, they seize the opportunity to take a corner more toward the inside, gaining on him.

I sent him messages on his dashboard, telling him Joseph and Kwan's lap times.

My heart palpitates during lap six as Kwan overtakes Julián. Being the fighter that he is, my Storm doesn't give up. With one Prima Pantera behind him and one in front, he's under even more pressure. He's not only defending his spot anymore, he's also trying to get the first place back.

I stop breathing between lap seven and eight because Julián is fighting Kwan, going side by side with him in the corner. I adjust his settings again when he's racing down the straight. I send him more updates on the others' laps and his tire degradation levels.

Three laps later, he takes corner four on a tighter line, overtaking Kwan again. He's back in first place, half the race over already.

His performance on the track, the lap times he's setting, it's remarkable. The Prima Pantera's are starting to struggle, but not Julián.

No.

He's speeding down the track as if his tires weren't losing grip little by little.

For the first time since the beginning of the race, he manages to create a bit of a gap, something I more than happily communicate with him over a message I send to his dashboard. He can probably see it at the sides of the track designated to displaying the gaps between the riders, but this way I can be sure he sees it.

Two laps before the end of the race, Julián is no longer under threat from the other competitors.

Hope expands in my chest, like air expands in a hot air balloon when it's heated. It's not something I can control, not that I want to. We're so close to winning our first race in MotoGP, so close to achieving what the media has called impossible since my husband became a rookie in this category of the sport.

He crosses the line again, starting the last lap of the race in first place for the first time this season.

My hand stays on my mouth for the first few corners, which is the only reason my gasp is muffled when halfway through the lap his zipper slides all the way down, exposing his chest.

"No, no, no," I mumble to myself, panicking because this is bad. Not only is Julián's safety at risk, but the stewards will *not* be happy with this.

"Fuck," I hear one of Julián's engineers curse beside me, and I throw her a worried look that she returns.

Wesley turns back to the screens and so do I, watching Julián cross the finish line and zipping his suit back up, waving his hands around in frustration. I can almost hear him screaming inside his helmet, cursing in English and Spanish. I know there are at least a couple "puñeta"s escaping him at the moment, and if I were the type of person to curse, I'd be right there with him.

"They're going to take this win for him as a punishment," Wesley says, pushing away from the desk we're sitting at with our screens. She's making her way toward the team principal of Hawke CWM, and I decide to follow her.

This isn't the first time a suit malfunction has caused a rider to lose their position by getting a penalty. It's always been unfair because it isn't the rider's fault. It's not as if they decide to undo their zipper and show off their chests. They would never do something so foolish and reckless.

Things like these happen by accident, and they shouldn't be punished.

And yet...

"The stewards are already discussing a five-place grid penalty," Sorena Erikson, the team principal, says before yelling at someone through the mouthpiece of her headphones.

I wait patiently for her to say anything else while also waiting for Julián to make his way back into the pitlane. My eyes stay trained on the entrance of it while Sorena keeps arguing with someone over the radio. I've met her a few times, shared several conversations with her, but she's usually a very calm and collected person who doesn't raise her voice. Right now, the tall woman with dark, curly hair and sharp facial features sounds ready to tear someone's head off.

I appreciate that.

It's what we need right now to ensure Julián doesn't lose his first win.

As soon as he makes his way to the first place sign, I step toward him. He's ripping off his helmet and balaclava as he storms toward me, completely ignoring the rest of his team. It's not to hug me or kiss me either, it's to ask me the one question we're both dreading to receive the answer to.

"Do I have to move my bike?"

Move it from the first place sign.

My heart sinks.

"I don't know. They're still talking about it," I explain.

His head sinks in defeat, and he finally wraps his arms around me. He smells like him combined with sweat and rubber, and he's wet from sweating, but I couldn't care less about any of that. I love him so much, and he's absolutely terrified that his best performance will no longer be his best performance because of a stupid zipper malfunction.

"As hot as you look with your racing suit half undone, maybe next time save it for when we're alone, baby," I whisper after several moments pass and he hasn't let me go yet.

"This would be a hell of a lot funnier if I wasn't so scared right now," he says, holding me tighter.

"I thought maybe picturing me naked would help."

"Well, it doesn't *not* help." I chuckle in response, feeling his shoulders untense a little. His hug becomes less rigid, and he melts into me.

Unfortunately, even while the stewards make up their minds, the post-race procedures must continue. Julián goes on to hug the rest of his team before grabbing his towel and water, downing half of it for hydration. His eyes keep skipping back to me, but I have to leave him eventually, desperate to get an update from Sorena or Wesley.

"What did they say?" I ask Sorena, and she shakes her head, furiously typing away on her laptop keys.

"They said they're going to look into this. For now, he's under investigation."

My stomach rolls at the thought of Julián accepting the trophy, celebrating this win, and later being stripped of it after they look through the data and information they have available. He will have to celebrate like none of that is happening in the background. He will have to put up a façade of happiness, but it will taint this moment forever, even if or when they decide he can keep this win.

I barely breathe past the tears that shoot into my eyes when I watch sadness cross Julián's face.

His joy is my joy.

His dreams are my dreams.

That means, his pain is my pain, which is why my chest hurts like someone punched me right in the heart.

Julián and I sit in his private room, waiting for the decision the stewards are still making. He's been clinging to me since he finished celebrating, showering, and then giving interviews. We haven't spoken much because there is nothing to say.

He's scared.

I'm scared.

What's the point of stating it?

If anything, it would only make both of us feel worse.

My eyes are stuck on the clock on the wall across from us, watching the seconds tick by. It makes my anxiety worse, but I can't look away.

Tick.

Tock.

Tick.

Tock.

Twenty more minutes pass before Julián breaks the silence.

"*Te quiero mucho, arcoíris. Con todo mi corazón. Con todo lo que tengo.*" My heart flutters happily at his words.

"*Te quiero más, mi amor.*" Julián shakes his head, tilting his head down while his thumb pushes my chin up to bring my mouth to his.

"*No es posible, esposa.*"

I smile right as he presses his lips to mine, but our moment is interrupted by his phone ringing. He leans back with a groan but since we're waiting for that phone call, he doesn't ignore it like he usually would when his mouth is on mine. Instead, he presses the phone to his ear with a shaky hand, listening to the person on the other end of the line speak.

My anxiety doubles as I watch Julián's stoic face remain unchanged throughout the whole conversation.

"Okay, I got it. Thanks for calling," he replies a minute later, hanging up as soon as the other person is finished talking. "I get to keep my first place," he says, and a wave of relief collides against the pit of dread in my stomach, sweeping away the negative feeling entirely.

"You've won your first race," I say, standing up when the nervous energy inside my body becomes too overpowering to keep sitting.

"I've won my first race," he repeats, getting up too so he can stand with me. "I did it."

"You did!" I leap into his arms, but he catches me with ease, holding me to him while his body shakes with a silent sob. Tears drip down my cheeks, and I hold onto his nape, tugging on his curls there.

"I think I'm going to pass out," he says, and I can't even blame him. The sudden weight lifting off my chest has also made a sense of lightheadedness creep in for me. I can only imagine the same is happening to him, maybe even on a more extreme level.

"I've got you, husband. I'm not letting go."

His arms tighten around me, holding onto me as if he's testing if my words are actually true.

He can test all he wants.

I have him.

And I'm never letting him go.

Chapter 11

Julián

It's been almost two months since I've won my first race.

Five more races have passed, and I won two more. Viktor has also won two, and Joseph took the other race. So far, we've stayed pretty close to each other in points, but I'm leading the championship. I'm in first place right now, and it's all the confidence boost I need to keep pushing as hard as I possibly can to win.

But not tonight.

Tonight is about my stunning wife and bringing her as much joy as absolutely possible.

"I would still like to know where you're taking me," she says because I've blindfolded her, which means for the last twenty minutes while I drove us to our location, Scar's had no way of even getting a hint.

We're in Austria at the moment for the thirteenth race of the season, and I've found the perfect place for us to spend the anniversary of our first "fake" date we had all those years ago.

"We're almost there, love. You can wait a little longer," I reply, and despite trying so hard to frown, her lips twitch until they eventually stretch into a smile.

"You can be very lucky you've made me enjoy your surprises over the years." My own smile spreads across my face at the thought of everything I've surprised her with so far.

A romantic boat tour on the Douro River in Portugal.

Several evenings with our house filled with lavender just because.

A new car because her old one was making unhealthy noises.

A trip to her grandparents' house in England where they moved a few years ago.

A trip to Puerto Rico where we visited some of my family.

Me in nothing but a bow covering my dick on her birthday.

The last one she really loved. She spent several moments simply staring at me, admiring me, before she took her time removing the bow with her teeth.

Pleasure runs down my spine in the shape of shivers at the reminder of that day.

It was a really good day.

"No bow tonight, wife," I say after I manage to wrestle back the memory to keep from getting hard at a very inappropriate time, but Scar's soft laugh has my whole body tensing.

"That's too bad. I rather enjoyed that."

With the key I was given, I open the door before leading her through them. We're at a roller rink location I found here in Austria, and I'm content when not a single person is in sight. They kept their promise to close it down for the evening, and I even paid a little extra to make sure all of the security cameras were turned off. To be extra sure, I had them sign a contract.

Which means, my wife and I are completely and utterly alone in here tonight, and I plan to make this evening special for her.

"Okay, I can smell popcorn. Did you bring me to a movie theater?" I can't help but chuckle.

"It's the anniversary of our first 'fake' date, and you think I brought you to the movies? It's like you don't know me at all," I tease, which makes her turn around in my hands to poke me in the stomach.

"Don't give me that. You took me to a movie theater for our first kiss anniversary."

"Only because they were showing the new Marvel movie and *you* said you were going, whether I was coming or not," I remind her, and she bursts into laughter in my arms.

My smile burns my cheeks, but there is no way it could fall while I watch her amusement take over every part of her body. I wish I could see her eyes right now, those sparkling blue ones that have had me on my knees since we met.

It's such a strong urge that I pull down her blindfold. I'd made sure to only tie it gently around her eyes so it didn't smudge her makeup, but a bit of mascara is still under her eyes. I wipe it away while she watches me, looking up at me with her heart in her gaze. I press a soft kiss to her lips, lingering for longer than I should, before finally turning her around to reveal the place we're standing in.

A place I've filled with lavender.

The lights are bright and colorful, giving the room an 80s vibe. The rink itself is surrounded by arcade games on the left side and a food area on the right. At the very back, there is the place where you get your shoes from, no one in sight there either. Our shoes are on the counter, along with a remote beside them with a sticky note on it, informing us to turn up the volume if we'd like.

Scar is carefully collecting all of the lavender she can reach without leaving my side, making a bigger bundle for herself. There are tears in her eyes, and as soon as I turn up the volume to let her hear 'Dancing Queen' by the Mamma Mia cast, one of her favorite movies of all time, they drip down her cheeks.

"You're such a jerk," she mumbles as she drops her face in her hands, and I immediately pull her into a hug.

"Does that mean you like it?" I kiss the top of her head while she lets out a breathless laugh.

"Of course I do. I love it, husband." She steps back to pull my head down and kiss me.

Scar doesn't linger though, not like I normally do.

No.

She picks up the skates, hands me mine, then moves toward the bench in front of the barrier of the rink to put on the shoes. It takes me a moment to stop staring at her, to stop admiring her, in order to sit beside my wife and start putting on the skates. I fumble with the laces for far longer than is attractive, until eventually Scar giggles and helps me undo the knot someone else had placed in it. Her nails are sharper than mine, so it takes her no time at all, which only makes her grin more.

"Don't laugh at me," I warn, and she bites down on her full bottom lip to keep it in. "I mean it, Scar. I'll spank your pretty ass if you do." My warning only makes her giggle before she fully laughs and skates away, onto the rink.

I finish tying my laces before chasing after her, catching her by her middle moments later. She squeals, and I laugh, a deep, full sound that I only ever expel when I'm around her.

Time seems to stand still and pass at lightning speed as we make our way around the rink over and over. The rest of the Mamma Mia soundtrack plays, and Scar is belting the songs from the top of her lungs.

I squeeze her ass a few times in a playful manner as I pass her, and she does the same to me whenever she's close enough.

My stomach starts to cramp from how much I'm laughing, especially when I fall on my ass because she poked me a little too close to the no-touch zone.

"I'm so sorry," she blurts out before dropping to her knees in front of me, still keeping a bit of distance.

The music changes as our laughter dies out.

No more Mamma Mia songs.

Instead, a song by *From Angels to Devils*, one of their slower, dirtier ones, fills the room. Scar's breathing is wonderfully uneven in the way it is when anticipation washes through her.

Mine mimics hers instantly.

"*Quiero que vengas gateando hasta aquí, mami.*" Scar's cheeks waste no time flushing a bright pink, which looks even brighter with the lights on her.

I lean back on my hands, watching my wife crawl to me with a shy smile on her lips. My eyes trail down from her face to her cleavage, admiring the way her neckline lets me see down her dress a little. I force my gaze back up to her face to see her bottom lip has slipped between her teeth.

When she's made her way between my legs, she runs her hands up my thighs, and my cock swells uncomfortably against my pants. A single look from Scar is usually enough to turn me on, but when she adds her hands to the mix?

I'm a goner.

"Cameras are turned off?" she asks, already going for the zipper on my jeans.

"Of course, love."

"No one's here."

"Made sure of it. Legally."

Scar slowly drags down my zipper, a painful tease that has my arms flexing as I restrain myself from reaching for it, guiding her onto her back, and speeding up this entire process so I can sink deep inside of her. But I know she likes foreplay. I know she likes the teasing, so I don't rush her.

Not yet.

"You planned this, didn't you? You knew I couldn't resist you if we were the only two people in here," she says, pushing my jeans to the side to reveal the way my hard cock is pressing against my boxers.

"No, *arcoíris*. I planned this because during our first 'fake' date, when we saw it was only the two of us at the rink, I wanted to rip off your dress. I wanted to worship your body with my mouth. I wanted to do so many things, but we weren't ready. We are now, and part of me was hoping we could recreate that day, this time with my fantasy playing out in real life, too."

The admission has a little moan escaping her, the sound like a lightning bolt of desire shooting straight through my system.

"I have to admit something to you, husband."

Scar leans forward, tilting my head back by pushing my chin up and back, to kiss along my neck. My nails dig into the floor as I continue to fight the urge to grab her hips, put her on her back, and spread her legs. The urge to make her come and come inside her at the same time.

"Admit it, *mami*. Let me hear it," I say as she continues to kiss up my neck, nipping my earlobe. Her right hand trails down my chest, toward my aching cock.

"I would have spread my legs for you without hesitation," she says and drops her hand all the way down to my groin, palming it roughly. "Because I wanted you—want you—just as badly."

Pleasure tightens everything inside of me, and I groan, but Scar kisses me, cutting off the sound. I push off the ground, thrusting into her hand in search of *more* while her tongue slips into my mouth.

Puñeta.

My self-control snaps entirely.

I break the kiss, lifting my hands into Scar's thick, dark hair. Pulling a little on it, just enough to get her head to tilt back without hurting her, I expose her neck to me.

Instead of kissing it like she did with me, I run the back of my fingers over the column of her throat. Scar loves being choked, so I tease her. Trail my fingers over her pulse point. Pressing down just enough to feel her racing heart. Using the tips of my fingers.

“Is that why you wore a sundress that day, wife? Because you would have let me slip my hand up your skirt?” I ask, but her response is a whimper when I brush my mouth over hers, just shy of kissing her. “Is that why you wore this pretty, purple sundress today?”

A moan escapes her when I finally wrap my hand around her throat and squeeze the sides in the way she likes.

“Yes, that’s why,” she pants out, her eyes fluttering shut. “Easy access,” she explains, and I chuckle as I release the hold on her hair. My hand cups her left breast, and my thumb plays with her nipple, feeling it pebble.

“Fuck, I love it when you don’t wear bras,” I say, putting my mouth back on hers while she arches her back to push her breast into my hand. She’s under my complete control, and it’s that trust, how safe she feels with me, that has me standing up and pulling her with me.

“Where are we going?” she asks, her eyes still mostly closed from the need inside of her. Need I can feel deep inside my chest, too.

I lead her to the railing enclosing the rink before slipping out of my shoes.

“Hold onto the railing, love.”

I love that she doesn’t even attempt to take her skates off. She leaves them on as she spins around, her hands grabbing the railing to do as she was told. Scar pushes her ass out and toward me, her sundress lifting until it barely covers her magnificent ass.

My mouth waters and my cock hardens even more at the sight.

“Touch me, Julián. Please.” My hands lift to her ass, cupping each cheek for a moment before lifting the dress.

Her panties are soaked, and when I slide them to the side, her pretty pussy is already swollen and needy for my touch.

I'm desperate to sink inside of her, but I also love making Scar come at least once before using my cock, so I drop to my knees behind her. My fingers are dirty, and there is no way in hell I'd risk fucking with Scar's health to make her come, especially when I've got a perfectly good mouth to get the job done.

I don't take my time tonight. I don't savor my time licking along the length of Scar's pussy. I eat her out like I haven't tasted her in years, going after her clit until she's shaking and quivering in my hands.

"Baby, oh my—"

She cuts off right as her orgasm slams through her, taking both of us by surprise. I suck on her clit as she shakes and shakes and shakes, her orgasm dragging on for a long time. My tongue stays on her pussy, licking along the length of it while she cries through her pleasure.

"Fuck," she curses, bucking against my mouth as she continues trembling. "That felt so good," my sweet wife says, giggling breathlessly. "I want more."

I trail kisses along her left ass cheek, spine, and pull her hair aside to kiss the back of her neck on my way to her ear.

"Yeah?" I ask, my fingers fumbling with my underwear to take my cock out, my mouth lingering by her ear.

"Yes," she replies, pushing her ass against me right as I free my cock. "I always want more of you." A moan escapes me when she rubs against my groin, sending more pleasure through me.

"You'll always get more of me, Scar. You will get as much as you want and can take, until your legs are shaking and you can't stand anymore. Until you're thoroughly satisfied." My words are followed by the head of my cock slipping inside of her, and she wastes no time clenching around me. For Scar, it's almost a reflex. It's the anticipation of getting all of me, but that also means I have to take my time.

No matter how wet she is, I can't thrust inside when she's tensing around me. It'll hurt her, and the only time we bring pain into the bedroom is when I'm spanking her for being a good girl. Yes, a good girl, because my wife loves being spanked and it's more of a reward than it is a punishment.

"Fuck, love, you're going to make me come in seconds if you keep squeezing me like this," I say and rub my hands along her ass cheeks, a gentle touch meant to relax her.

"I don't want that. I want you to fuck me so hard you'll have to carry me out of this place."

Scar's filthy mouth is one of my many weaknesses.

It has me gripping her ass harder, spreading her wider as I push a little further inside of her. She's relaxing now like she's welcoming me in, so I push all the way inside until I'm completely buried in her.

"Fuuuuuck," I groan as Scar moans loudly enough to fill the whole place with that wonderful sound.

"You feel so good. You always feel so good," Scar says, bouncing a little on my cock when I don't move.

As much as I love being inside her without a condom, without anything between us, sometimes I have a hard time not coming from the mere sensation of her warmth, her feel. Her.

"Please move, husband. I need to come," she says, and I squeeze her wide hips before dropping my hands to her ass to spread her open for me. I want to watch myself slide in and out of her because the way we fit together is one of my favorite things in the world.

"So greedy." I pull out to drive back inside of her, hard and fast like she enjoys. "But you beg so pretty, love, so I could never deny you a single thing, let alone feeling you come around my cock."

My words have her moaning so loudly, my eyes roll into the back of my head as a wave of pleasure bursts through me.

My thrusts are sloppy and fast, both of us chasing the bliss of our orgasms. Scar shifts back to meet every single one of my pumps, and I dig my fingers into her hips to hold onto reality as everything inside of me tenses. I fuck into her hard and fast, then slow and soft. I go shallow to hit her G-spot before going as deep as possible, groaning with every single thrust.

My balls pull tight and then I'm coming, no longer able to hold off to make sure she falls apart, too.

But Scar knows exactly how to use me while I'm still hard inside of her, my cock pulsing and filling her with my cum. My legs are shaking, so she bounces on my dick, moaning and crying out in pleasure as she finally comes again too.

It's worth the overstimulation that has my entire body twitching.

Both of us are entirely out of breath by the time reality comes crashing back in, and I enjoy the way we stay connected even as Scar stands upright, pressing her back to my front. Her dress is bunched up around her waist, her panties still pushed to the side to keep me buried inside her.

"We should spend all anniversaries this way," Scar says as I run my hands over her round stomach, tracing the stretchmarks near her hips.

"Fucking at a roller rink?" She giggles, and I can't help the smile blooming on my face.

"Well, more trying out new things *like* fucking at a roller rink," she corrects, and I burst into laughter.

"You make me so, so happy, love. Do you know that?" I kiss her cheek, holding her close to me.

"I know. Hopefully as happy as you make me."

It's on the tip of my tongue to argue that I'm the happiest man in the world because of her and there is nothing I could ever do to match this feeling for her, but who am I to determine that for her?

That's not the kind of man I want to be.

That's not the kind of husband I am.

"I love you," is what I respond instead, tilting her head to the side to claim her mouth.

Chapter 12

Julián

There are six races left in the season, including the one in Japan in a week's time.

I'm leading the championship by a tiny eleven-point lead that could be taken away during any race weekend if I were to crash again. Like I did in Catalonia. Viktor has been so consistent, it's impossible to create a bigger gap between us in the standings. Not to mention, the Prima Pantera racers are on our asses too.

It's a mess.

My father's company has been steady for now, but the bank's insistent on getting the money we owe back as soon as possible. We've been able to pay off little amounts to keep them happy for now, thanks to Elias' investment plans slowly paying back some money, but it's nowhere near enough.

Nothing we can pull off will be enough except for the prize money when I win the title.

"Julián, could you zip me up?"

My head shoots up from my phone where I'm looking over the million emails I've received in the past twenty-four hours. My heart stutters at the sight of Scarlette, the love of my life, standing in the middle of our hotel room in a white dress with lavender painted along the hem of it. The straps are loosely hanging down her arms because the dress isn't zipped up yet, and I find myself jumping to my feet to close the distance between us. She lifts her long, dark hair and spins to reveal her bare back to me.

I run a single finger down her spine, watching shivers appear in response to my touch.

"I asked you to zip me up, not turn me on, husband." Her words are soft and a little breathless.

I don't respond. Instead, I very slowly drag up her zipper while my other hand runs along the side of her body, feeling the fabric tighten around her generous curves. The sundress has a corset style at the top and is loose and flowy from her waist down. When she turns in my arms, I see that it has pushed up her breasts in a way that makes my mouth water, but it's her face that has me breathless.

Those blue eyes, full lips, and the scar running down her mouth. She's wearing more makeup than she usually is, highlighting all of her beautiful features.

"We have to get to the charity event. They're probably waiting for us already," she says but kisses me so deeply, the entire room spins by the time she steps back.

"Hmmmm," is the only thing I manage to reply because my head is all woozy from her kiss, following her out the door to go to the event our friends have invited us to today.

"Scarlette, I'm so happy to see you again!"

Valentina Romana's voice travels through the space of the venue as she very gracefully runs toward my wife with her arms extended. Scar's entire face lights up at the sight of the current Velocità Rossa reserve driver and future Alfa Adrenalina F1 driver. She's in a dress as yellow as sunflowers, and her boyfriend is right behind her in a matching dress shirt with the sleeves rolled up. Gabriel Biancheri's gaze is attached to Valentina the way I know mine is to Scarlette most of the time.

From what Scar has told me, they only recently got back together after they broke up for reasons Valentina didn't share with Scar.

I know far more about these people than I am comfortable with.

"*Hola*, Julián. *Es un placer volver a verte*," Valentina says in flawless Spanish, catching me a bit off-guard.

"*El placer es mio*," I reply politely, trying to play nice with the future F1 driver my wife will be the race engineer for. Valentina offers me an intrigued smile and tilts her head, inspecting my expression.

"You're mad at me for taking Scar away, aren't you?" she asks, and her expression turns shy and apologetic. Not regretful, though, and I don't fault her for that. I'd have fought for Scar, too, if I didn't know that being an F1 race engineer is her dream.

"Not at all. This is what Scar's been working toward," I reply with complete honesty, which doesn't seem to make any sense to Valentina.

"But you look like you want to bite my head off."

"Don't worry, *bella*, that's just his face." Chiara Tick says and places a comforting hand on Valentina's shoulder. Her belly is a lot more swollen than it was the last time I saw her, but she still adds, "But if he ever did try to bite your head off, I'd rip his off instead," and scowls at me threateningly.

I don't doubt that, even while pregnant, Chiara Tick could beat my ass more effortlessly than anyone else in the world.

"My sunflower could defend herself, Chiara," Gabriel chimes in, wrapping his arms around Valentina from behind. She smiles and melts into him, looking more at peace than I've ever seen a person look.

"It's Mrs. Tick to you, Gabriel." She glares at him, turning his cheeks red before he hides his face in his girlfriend's neck.

I'm guessing Chiara hasn't warmed up to him again since everything happened. It almost makes me smile to see the Italian woman so protective.

"Sweetheart, you have to get me out of here. I'm about to adopt all of these puppies, and Benz is not going to be happy to get several new siblings in the span of a few months. She's already going to hate having to share the spotlight with our little girl," Leonard says as he approaches his wife, placing a hand on her hip and slowly sliding it onto her stomach.

"Hosting this event and attending was *your* idea," she reminds him, but Chiara is smiling as he turns her around to lead her to where some of the youngest puppies are playing in a pen. Scarlette and Valentina follow them, and Gabriel, being attached to Valentina's side, walks with them.

I have about a moment of silence before the bane of my peace approaches.

"Hey, Storm, it's nice to see you, man." My head falls backward and I almost let out a sigh.

"I didn't know you were also going to be here," I mumble when Adrian steps in front of me, preventing me from seeing Scar and Valentina.

"Fuck, that's awful. You couldn't even look forward to it."

His arrogant smile and cocky words almost bring out my smile, and it irritates me because, while I know I like him far more after our night at the club, he's still insufferable most days.

"Dread it, you mean," I correct him, but the Monegasque has the audacity to laugh in my face.

"This whole enemies-to-lovers thing always ends up with the people falling in love with each other, Storm. My sister has explained enough plots of her books to me. So, I'd be careful." He winks at me before walking away, and now that he's finally out of sight and hearing range, I let out the chuckle I've been holding back.

"I heard that," Leonard Tick says as he approaches me again, taking up the space Adrian was occupying mere moments ago.

"You heard nothing." Leonard smirks, and I'm so taken aback, I forget to be upset with him.

"You can try to be a grumpy wanker all you want around Adrian Romana, trust me I've tried, but eventually, that man is going to force his way into your heart. Don't try to fight it. Having someone like Adrian looking out for you is a blessing, not a curse," he says, his accent thicker than I've ever heard before.

"But he's got such a—" I cut off, trying to look for a good way to describe him.

"A loud personality," Leonard finishes for me, nodding in agreement. "Yeah, you're right. But he's got an even bigger heart, and that's what's important. I mean, look at him."

The Brit steps to the side to gesture toward where Adrian is now on the floor, four puppies ruining what I'm assuming are very expensive pants and an even more expensive shirt. He's smiling from ear to ear as he dotes on the puppies, giving them love and attention.

"He really is just pure sunshine, isn't he?" I ask, and Leonard places his hand on my shoulder, squeezing it gently.

"He is, but much like the dogs I'm throwing this event for, he's lost and desperate for any type of love people are willing to give him."

He drops his hand, and I look around the room, watching the dogs of all ages and sizes in those tiny cages look at the people walking past them with eyes that scream, "Please, take me with you. I don't want to be imprisoned here anymore."

My heart sinks, and the sensation seems to call Scar to me because she closes the distance between us and takes my hand.

"I know, I feel the same way." She kisses my cheek before guiding me toward where Valentina is now standing with Gabriel, Chiara, Leonard, and Cameron Kion.

My eyes stay on all of the dogs as the group of friends converse, and I especially can't look away from the two Bernese Mountain dogs that are together in one kennel. They're cuddling in the corner, no one even looking their way, which is I'm guessing because they're already all grown up unlike the other puppies here.

Leonard threw this charity event and invited as many people as could fit in here comfortably. He's doing that more and more now to both fund shelters but also get the dogs out. He's very particular about which shelters he sponsors because some of them are very problematic, but he's told me he's working on putting those out of business and relocating the animals they keep there to shelters that won't euthanize them for simply existing.

My heart aches all over again.

Before I can stop them, my feet start moving of their own accord, taking me toward the Bernese Mountain dogs. I squat down in front of the bars that keep them separated, feeling the urge to rip that metal off its hinges to free them.

"Hey, you two," I say and they waste no time coming toward me with their tails swishing from side to side. They both sniff my hand, then the one on the left—the one who has a much bigger head and is drooling far more than the one on the right—starts crying and wagging even more as it comes closer to the bars. The other one, the smaller one with significantly less white painted on its nose and head, is shier, keeping its distance from me now that the other one is throwing itself toward me.

"You're the first person all day to pay them any attention," someone says from beside me, and I look up to see a tall person with grey hair, light brown skin, and dark brown eyes staring down at me with a soft smile.

"How old are they?" I ask, and they turn to pick up a chart on a clipboard to hand to me.

"All of the information is on there," they say. "The one on the left is Diablo. The one on the right is Jax. They've both been here for over a year, dropped off because the family moved to another country and didn't want to take them."

I hate people.

I hate humanity.

I hate that while that story is awful, I bet some of the other dogs here have an even worse one.

My eyes carefully scan all of the information on the sheet of paper in my hands. Jax is six years old, and Diablo is three. They've been together since the family got Diablo three years ago, and they can't be separated. Apparently, they're playful, good-natured, and love people. They're tri-colored—brown, white, and black—and both of them have beautiful brown eyes that they're currently using to look at me with so much sadness, I can no longer hold the tears back.

"I'm so sorry they didn't take you with them. I can't understand how anyone could possibly leave you behind," I tell them, a tear rolling down my cheek as Jax finally approaches me too, letting me pet his head.

"Julián, are you okay, baby?" More tears stream down my face at the sound of Scar's voice.

"No, I'm not. Look at them, Scar. They're so sweet and they need a good, loving home that's never going to put them in a shelter," I say, still petting Diablo's head.

"A home like ours?" she asks as she squats down beside me. Diablo immediately goes toward her, pushing his big snout through the bars to sniff her.

"Yes."

The word is out of my mouth before I even process what this would mean for us.

"They could stay with your mom on the weekends we can't take them with us. She's been talking about getting a dog for months. She will probably be very happy to help. Not to mention, in less than two months, we're going to be home a lot, so we can spend all our time with them." My head snaps her way, surprise infiltrating my body.

"You've really thought about this, haven't you?" My wife smiles softly at me.

"Baby, I haven't just thought about this. I've spoken to your mom, who has already agreed this would be a good idea. I've spoken to Elias and Vi, who would love to introduce Liliana to dogs, too," she says and takes my face in her hands when more tears stream down my cheeks. "I knew as soon as we'd step into this place, we'd find one—" She cuts off to look at the two Berners. "—or two angels we'd want to take home. It wasn't a matter of if this was going to happen, simply when."

I love her so much.

It's something I remember every minute I'm in her presence, but it's moments like these when I *really* understand how much I love her. Because she knows me so well. And on top of that, she matches me with every stride I take. We fit together so well, there is no question about whether we were made for each other. Of course, we were. We're more than two puzzle pieces that fit together.

We are like lavender and bees.

We need each other to grow, to survive.

It's more than simply fitting together.

It's belonging together.

"This whole life thing would be so very bleak without you, *arcoíris*." Scar kisses me gently before turning back to Diablo and Jax.

They're both wagging, and Diablo is still crying for more attention.

I'm only happy to give it to him.

"You can go in to spend some time without the barrier in the way," the same person from before tells us about ten minutes later, and I look up at them, my hands completely covered in slobber and hair.

It's wonderful and disgusting at the same time.

"We'd love that," Scar answers for us, and I barely manage to pull my hands away from the babies long enough to walk through the door and into their enclosure.

As soon as Scar and I are inside, Diablo throws himself against our legs, something I know dogs do to hug. Jax is still a bit shy, but he approaches, too, wagging a little less than his brother. He's definitely more distrusting, and I wonder what happened to him that made him feel like he needs to have all of his walls up around people.

Like me.

"Hey, sweetheart. It's okay," Scar says before lifting her dress a little to kneel down on the floor.

"Love, your dress is going to get full of dog hair," I warn, but Scar simply shrugs.

"Couldn't care less," she replies and holds out her hand for Jax. He sniffs her hand now that she's inside of his space, then moves even closer to sniff her mouth, right where her scar is.

Part of me wonders what it would be like if he could sniff it and see the memory in Scar's head at the same time, the memory of that very dark day that she doesn't like to remember. Another part likes to believe that maybe he can sense something, anything, and that's why he's spending so much time sniffing the area.

"Dogs are really good for people with anxiety. Did you know that?" she asks me when Jax nudges her chin with his snout.

"I did," I reply, smiling down at the image of the two of them while also petting Diablo's head.

Every time I stop, he throws his paw at me, demanding more. Before we went in here, whenever I attempted to pet his brother, he threw his head into my hand to get me to love on him instead.

He's a needy one, that's for sure.

"This is perfect. Two, so we each have one to give attention to and no one feels left out," Scar says while giggling when Jax licks her chin and wags even more.

Life with you is perfect.

Chapter 13

Scarlette

Diablo has more than proven why he was given his name.

He's a little devil but in the cutest way imaginable.

While Jax is calm and behaves like an absolute angel, Diablo is energetic and wreaks havoc around the house. He's a bit clumsy in everything he does, and I love him so much already, even if he's accidentally ripped down several curtains and broken some blinds to make what we call "peepholes" for himself so he can watch the people that walk by our house.

Jax mostly sleeps, as Bernese Mountain dogs are supposed to, unless Diablo starts barking at people that walk by. Then, they both start a concert of barking and howling until the people are no longer near our house.

Both of them are huge fans of ice cubes, Diablo even more so than Jax. The little—in age but much bigger in size—guy comes running every time he hears the fridge popping out iced cubes.

Julián's and my main goal as dog parents is to give them the longest, happiest lives from now on that they could have. They give us so much love and loyalty in return, it's the very least we can do.

"Do you think bringing them to the office when you have a meeting with the board members is a good idea?" I ask as Diablo drags me to yet another patch of grass outside of Julián's company's building to mark his territory.

"Well, Elias is bringing Liliana, and he asked me to get them here so she could meet them. Plus, it's my building, which means I get to do whatever I want to do."

He says it as if he hadn't sent out an email to all of the employees on his level of the building to ensure none of them are scared of big dogs. Only after they all emailed back, confirming they weren't afraid, did Julián tell me we were taking the dogs.

My husband may be in charge, but he's still the kindest man I've ever met. Grumpy as heck, yes, but he's got the best soul.

Diablo and Jax are both unsure of the elevator, but with a lot of treats and even more praise, they make it onto it. Diablo is sniffing the entire space while Jax stays glued to Julián's side which he's been for the last week since we came back from Indonesia where my husband came in second in the race. Julián won the race in Japan, extending his championship lead.

He's on track to save his father's company. He's so close to achieving what he's so desperate to accomplish.

"I hate these fucking meetings," Julián grumbles as soon as we reach the correct level, Diablo immediately running around the space when I unleash him. He's a big teddy bear who loves people, so he's going to be busy for the next three hours simply getting all of the attention the people in the office are willing to give him.

"I know, husband."

"I hate all of this dress-up shit, pretending to care about what those assholes have to say," he adds in a quiet whisper, making sure I'm the only person who can hear him talk so badly about the board members.

"I don't blame you. They all have a stick up their butts." He chuckles at my choice of words.

"That they do, love." He takes my hand in his, and we stroll toward Elias' office where he's waiting with Vi and Liliana. "I just hope they'll be happy with how I've performed this season in MotoGP so they can finally get off Elias' back a little. He's suffering so much."

"With a newborn baby and trying to keep the company afloat long enough for the money of your win to come in, I'd be surprised if he isn't suffering."

They both are.

Julián has been since he found out that his dad's company is in debt. He's struggled so much trying to carry this weight on his shoulders. A weight I can't share with him because even if I take part of it on myself, Julián does everything in his power to take it back onto his shoulders so I don't suffer, too. What he doesn't seem to understand is that I will always be in pain with him, just like I will always share his joy and everything else he's feeling. That's part of being married to your soulmate, your other half.

As soon as we step inside Elias' office, Diablo following us even though he hasn't finished his round around the office space, my heart warms at the sight of my niece holding tightly onto Vi's hair.

Julián releases my hand because he knows I have one singular priority when I see Liliana, and that is to cuddle her and kiss her round cheeks until she's smiling.

"Hi, sweet girl," I say as Violet lets me take her out of her arms, but the little baby is already reaching for me and smiling when I start complimenting how cute she is with my baby voice.

"I'm not going to get her back any time soon," Vi tells her husband, but he merely chuckles.

I don't want to have kids. It was a decision I've made from the time I was old enough to understand what it meant not to have children, not fitting into those societal standards. The world tells women they need to have children, that it is their purpose in life, but it's never been mine. I've always wanted to be an aunt to Vi's kids. She used to tell me how many children she wanted with the right person and, while I didn't understand why, I always told her I'd be there by her side to love her children with my whole heart because they would be part of her. And I love my best friend wholeheartedly.

"You're the cutest baby ever," I coo to Liliana, who is still smiling and squealing when I kiss her cheek and blow air against it, making a farting noise.

"I think Diablo just took personal offense to that statement, *arcoíris*." I turn to see Diablo looking at me with big, brown eyes, looking every shade of unhappy.

"She's the cutest *human* baby," I correct, and he wags his tail as if he truly understood every single word coming out of my mouth. Maybe he's just happy to see I'm looking at him, talking to *him*, but I'd like to believe he understands me.

I catch Julián smiling at me and flash him one in return.

"*Ay, puñeta,* Storm," Elias blurts out and jumps out of his chair. "We're going to be late." He's rushing out of the door before his best friend has a chance to respond, and Julián stares after him for a second with furrowed brows.

"He does know I own this company, right?" he asks Vi and me, but Violet is already on the couch with Diablo now sitting beside her, staring up at her for attention. She doesn't give him any because her eyes are closed as she attempts to catch up on the months of sleep she's missing while I take care of Liliana.

"Have a good meeting," I say and meet my husband in the middle of the room so he can give me the kiss he always places on my lips when he leaves.

"Don't drop the baby," he replies, and I smack his stomach for the horrible joke.

He chuckles as he kisses me, then walks out the door. I admire his ass in those dress pants he's wearing before trailing my eyes up to watch how his dress shirt, wonderfully fitted to his body, shows off his back muscles.

Liliana drags my attention to her with a sound that is a combination of a laugh and squeal, and I notice she's looking at where Jax is playing with one of the toys Julián placed on the ground for both of them.

"Let's go play with the doggies while your uncle and daddy deal with those boring people." She giggles again, and I hug her to my side, holding onto her tightly.

CHAPTER 14

Julián

All of the board members are already seated around the long, rectangular table, waiting for me to take my seat at the head of it. I smooth a hand down my tie and take a deep breath, trying to make it subtle enough so no one notices how uncomfortable I am.

The board is made up of ninety percent of old, white men, something I know Elias was trying to change for years without success. Unfortunately, they are the ones with the most money that signed contracts under my dad that we could not unravel, no matter how hard we tried because I didn't want to own a company that was not inclusive. I didn't want to deal with these people who are so set in their ways. Then again, I didn't want any of this.

Not this company.

Not fighting for it because it was going downhill.

But it's my father's legacy, so who the fuck am I to throw everything he built away simply because I don't agree with it?

He'd be so disappointed in me if I'd do that.

"We have called this meeting to discuss the offer our biggest rival company, Aeroplane Parts, have made us," Julius Wade, the oldest member of the board and the one who has been here the longest, says. He looks like a typical sixty-five-year-old white man with a full beard and thinning white hair.

"An offer for what?" I ask through gritted teeth, suspicious of what the fuck he has to say now.

He's hated that my father left me his company ever since he found out I'd be the owner and put Elias in charge as CEO. Julius has made that abundantly clear from my first day, and he's not trying to hide his distaste for me now either. He flashes me a disgusted scowl, and if getting rid of him as a board member wasn't so damn expensive, I'd throw him out onto the street right now.

"To buy our company and make it a subsidiary of theirs."

My heart drops all the way into my stomach.

"We can't do that. We can't sell it to Aeroplane Parts. My father hated them," I say, pointing at absolutely nothing in front of me. Julius' eyes sparkle with the anger for me he harbors deep inside.

"We can, and if the majority of the board votes for it, then we will." Everyone else at the table stays completely silent, even my best friend, but I can't fault him for that. By the way the color has drained from his face and his mouth hangs agape, I can tell this is the first time he's hearing about this too.

"I'm still the owner of this company. I—"

"You are nothing. You are a nepo baby who inherited this company after your father died. You don't want to be here, and frankly, we don't want you in charge anymore either. Everything that happens at the company is relayed to you with a delay because you are always too busy playing with your motorcycles to truly care about the future of this place. So, respectfully, Mr. Alvarez, you may own this company, but we are the ones who have kept it afloat while your best friend fucked everything up. Our money has been drained because of his damn environmentally friendly solutions that cost us a fortune." My mouth seals shut because, really, what am I going to say to that?

He's not wrong. I hate that he isn't, but arguing for the sake of defending my hurt pride is ridiculous.

"That is why when we sell, you will sell your shares with it. Aeroplane Parts has requested that your shares be sold. You will get a lot of money out of this, money you can use to leave Moonville. I heard from your best friend over there that that was your plan before you inherited this company all those years ago anyway, so now is your chance."

It takes everything in me not to let the tears collect in my eyes.

They're kicking me out.

They're forcing me out of my dad's company.

They're *selling it to our rivals, to the one company my father never wanted to sell to.*

This can't be happening.

My head starts to spin as my breathing turns shallow. Panic grips my throat, and I have to hold onto my knees as tightly as possible to keep myself centered so I don't fall off the chair. Maybe it's not my head that's spinning, maybe it's the entire world that is suddenly spinning faster. Maybe it's also refusing the fact that the second worst thing possible is happening to my father's legacy right now.

I'm going to be sick.

"We will vote by a show of hands. All those in favor of selling?" Julius says, and I realize that they all knew. Every single hand but Elias' lifts in the air, and I know this was a setup. They discussed this before they requested this meeting. They got all of the information, probably from Julius, and they've been plotting this for a long time.

"I've been working my ass off this entire season to get us the money we need to pay off the debt this company is in, and this is how you thank me? By kicking me out?" I ask, feeling more and more sick by the second.

"Yes, this is how we thank you, you ungrateful brat. If you'd been here, if you hadn't spent all your time chasing an impossible dream, we wouldn't do this to you, but we can't have an owner that doesn't give a shit about this company." The tears finally shoot into my eyes, and I swallow hard to keep them from dropping down my cheeks.

"You will get your money as soon as this deal closes. You can finally be free of the responsibilities you didn't want to have to begin with, Julián." This comes from another man, the second oldest man at the table. His name is Timothy Hagel. He's kind. At least he used to be kind to me when I was a child and my father brought me here.

"You know he wouldn't have wanted this," I say, but my voice is pathetically weak from the pain spreading through my chest. I stare into Timothy's eyes, but he gives me a compassionate look that only makes me sicker.

"He wouldn't have wanted you to suffer in this place, either."

I shake my head and push away from the table, trying to keep my hands from shaking.

"I hope you all remember that by doing this, you destroy everything my father, a man you called 'friend,' built." I'm on my way out of the room when Julius' voice stops me.

"No, son, you destroyed it when you tried to turn it into something it wasn't."

That's my final straw.

My tears finally drop down my cheeks, but I don't let anyone see. I storm out of that room and straight toward Elias' office, hoping Scar didn't go anywhere. My heart is racing, and I'm fighting a full breakdown with every fiber of my strength.

I'm almost by her side.

I've almost made it to my wife.

Then, I can fall apart.

I just have to get to her.

My feet carry me as fast as they can while everything continues to spin, my stomach rolls, and all feeling leaves my legs because of the lack of oxygen flowing through my limbs. My vision blurs, too, but that's mostly from the amount of tears that are filling my eyes too quickly to be shed. I stumble through the halls, trying to keep from throwing up my breakfast because the grief inside of me is too strong, too overwhelming, for my body to process or handle. It's trying to claw its way out of me, and I barely hold it back by humming, a trick that Scar taught me to fight nausea.

I burst through the door and shut it quickly, making both women in the room snap their heads my way. Diablo and Jax run toward me, too, and I allow myself to finally sink to my knees and break down.

"Julián? Baby, what happened?"

I hear her voice, but all I manage is to drop my face into my hands and start crying even harder, sobbing like I did the day my dad died. Because this feels the very same. Losing this company feels like losing him all over again, a second wave of grief I never expected to have to feel. I thought the initial pain would never return, but what he built here is what I held onto to feel connected to him, and now that's gone too.

I have no more connection to my father.

Because I wasn't good enough.

I didn't spend enough time at the company.

I let it get to the point where the board thought the only way to save it was by selling it.

"I lost it. I ruined everything," I cry into my hands, the words hardly audible.

Two snouts poking my hands, and I'm pretty sure Diablo licks my cheek where it's exposed and the tears are trailing down. I don't move because I can't feel any part of my body until Scar's hands wrap around my wrists to let me know she's there.

She doesn't try to pull my hands from my face, doesn't force me to do anything. Simply tells me she's there, and that's all I need to find the strength in me to take a deep breath.

"What happened?" Scar repeats after several moments of me trying to calm down by breathing deeply over and over.

It takes me another moment before I'm able to drop my hand to look into those bright-blue eyes of hers. They're full of concern, and I know she's trying her best to keep her anxiety at bay, anxiety born from uncertainty.

From the pain inside of me.

From seeing me shatter and break apart for the second time since we met.

It hurts me even more that I'm doing this to her. I don't want to make her worry or anxious, or both for that matter, but my vocal cords feel tied together. I'm trying to respond to take away the uncertainty hanging in the air, but staring into her eyes, though it settles me, doesn't loosen my stuck tongue.

She will be so sad when she hears that all of our work this season has been for nothing. All of the pressure we've been carrying to win the championship *was for nothing*. It could have been prevented if only they made this decision earlier.

And yet, they waited until there were only four races left to tell me it was all a waste of my fucking time.

"They're selling the company, and they're kicking me out."

CHAPTER 15

Scarlette

Julián has been strangely… calm for the past week.

He's also been quieter than he usually is with me, but I haven't pushed him to tell me what's going through his head.

I know he needs some time to process everything, and it's not fair of me to demand answers to the million questions I have swirling around in my head while he figures himself out. Plus, I think he wants to focus on the fourth to last race of the season here in Australia.

Diablo and Jax came with us considering now, after the board signed the deal and made Julián sign it, we're millionaires who can afford to get a private jet. Usually, Julián would have never spent money this way, but he didn't want to leave our babies at home this time, so he organized a jet to take them. Halo also came with us this week, but he's been mostly minding his own business, wandering around Melbourne to do some sightseeing before he joins me for the weekend in the garage.

"*¿Quieres ir conmigo, mi arcoíris*?" Julián says as he peeks his head through the door of our hotel room where I'm sitting on the floor with Diablo and Jax, putting on some makeup.

"*¿A donde*?" I ask with a smile, putting down my mascara to look at him.

All I get in response is a sweet smile, a rare sight these days.

I'm on my feet within a second.

The four of us walk along the beach at Port Melbourne, enjoying the spring weather that Melbourne has to offer at this time of the year. It's sixty-eight degrees Fahrenheit, a wonderful change from the fifty-five we're currently dealing with in Moonville.

The wind is warm, the sun hugs our skin like a comforting blanket, and Diablo and Jax are having the time of their lives playing in the water. It's still too cold for my liking, but the two Berners don't care about the temperature. In fact, I think they love getting cooled down.

Julián spreads out the towel he brought for us while we each hold onto one of the long leashes that let Diablo and Jax play in the water even though we're sitting a little further away from where the tide is coming in. My husband reaches for my free hand, and I look up at him to see the thoughtful expression covering his features.

"*Dime, mi amor. Sé que quieres decirme algo.*" I can read it on his face now that we're here, having our peaceful moment. He needs to get his thoughts, the ones he keeps spiraling into, off his chest, so he can creep out of the darkness.

"I lost his legacy," he says, dropping his head and shaking it a little. I bring my hand to his nape, cupping it gently and running my thumb over it.

"I know you think that company was your dad's legacy, baby, but it wasn't," I say, holding onto the leash a bit tighter when Diablo attempts to go further into the water. Julián turns his head my way, and I take advantage of this new position to cup his cheek, tracing his birthmark with my finger as I study his two differently-colored eyes.

"Then what is?" he asks, furrowing his brows.

"Isn't it obvious?" I press my thumb to his lips and run it over them, memorizing their shape over and over. "You are, Julián 'Storm' Alvarez. You are your father's legacy. You're the very best parts of him, and if he was here, he'd be so proud of everything you have accomplished for yourself. He'd want you to be happy, and you were never happy at his company to begin with."

Tears fall down his cheeks, and I wipe them away with the back of my fingers.

"I know you wanted to save his company. I know you feel like you failed. But you didn't," I say and suck in a sharp breath. "Can I say something not so great?"

"You can say whatever you want. You know that." He kisses the palm of my hand, shifting his gaze to Jax and Diablo to check that they're still okay.

"I think them paying you out, you no longer being the owner of the company you never wanted, is a relief to you. One you don't want to allow to sink in because it'll make you feel like an even worse son than you already do. But it is a relief. Deep down, I know you're glad you don't have to pretend to care about that place anymore because you know that's not what would have made your dad proud. He would have been proud seeing you accomplish your dreams."

Julián sinks further into my touch as he listens attentively, and even when I'm done speaking, he doesn't argue. Part of me was scared he would tell me I'm wrong, that I don't know him as well as I think I do, but I shouldn't doubt the connection between us.

I'm right.

He knows it.

I know it.

I'm pretty sure Elias would tell him the same thing, but the two of them are not speaking a lot at the moment. Elias is busy trying to adjust to this new phase of his career, and Julián is avoiding his best friend to keep from hearing about what's happening to his father's company right now.

"If I admit that I'm relieved, I will be the worst and most ungrateful child in the history of ungrateful and horrible children."

“You see, that’s where I disagree with you. I think it would finally set you free to admit you never wanted this in the first place and that you’re glad it’s over with so you can focus on your career,” I say and loop my arm through the leash to grab Julián’s face in both of my hands. “It’s okay to be relieved. It doesn’t make you a bad son. Allow yourself to finally let go,” I add, and his breathing hitches as he takes a deep breath. He lets it out shakily, more tears falling down his face.

“I’m relieved,” he whispers, leaning forward to press his forehead to mine. “I’m so relieved,” he repeats, this time with a firmer, louder voice.

“I’m proud of you.”

I kiss him gently before burying myself in his side, letting his arm envelop me and hold me tightly as we watch our babies continue to play in the water. They’re having the best time simply jumping in and out of the water, playing with each other. They don’t need toys when they have each other’s company.

The afternoon sun is slowly setting, and as it leaves, the wind starts to feel much colder than it did when we first left our hotel to walk along Port Melbourne’s beach. Julián, noticing immediately, takes off his sweatshirt and puts it on me instead. I wasn’t even shivering or complaining about the dip in temperature. He simply acted without thinking twice about his own comfort.

So very Julián.

“There is something else I’d look to discuss with you, love,” he says once we make our way back to the hotel, Diablo and Jax both dripping wet from playing in the water. Diablo keeps shaking and Jax is happily carrying the stick he found on the beach like a proud trophy.

I’m already dreading having to take it away from him before we go up to our room.

“Sounds serious,” I reply with a grin that makes him smile.

"It is a little," he admits, lacing his fingers through mine to bring me closer to him. "I know we were discussing moving to somewhere in Europe a few months ago, but I think the best place to go is Monaco. You'll have to be there a lot for work next year, and I can easily travel to other places in Europe from there. Elias and Violet would like it there as well, I think, so that's what I've been thinking about. Moving to Monaco."

With the money we've just received and both of our incomes, we could live comfortably there. And he's right. For work next year, it would be much better for me. Plus, Valentina lives there, and Chiara was telling me she was thinking about moving there as well to open another art gallery in Monaco. All my friends would be there on top of it being a suitable place to live for Julián's and my work, which is probably where my next words come from.

"I think that's a really good idea."

Nothing is keeping me in Moonville. The thought of putting more distance between my parents and me is quite appealing as well, especially ever since I didn't invite them to our wedding. I don't speak to them much anymore. I used to have a good relationship with my mother, but the older I got, the clearer it became that my life, no matter how important she claimed it was to her, was never more important than her own. She made everything about herself, and Julián showed me I deserved better than to be treated like that.

He showed me what true, unconditional, and pure love was.

"Anywhere we go together sounds like a wonderful place to me," I add and wrap my arms around one of his, placing my head on his shoulder.

"I'm glad you like the idea because I've been looking at houses, and I think I may have found our dream home," he says with a mischievous grin, one that I see when I tilt my head back to look at him.

"You've already looked for houses?" I'm not in the least bit annoyed. On the contrary, I think it's adorable that my husband is so invested in finding us a beautiful house to make our home.

"Of course. I've already looked at companies to ship our furniture, bikes, and cars as well." My cheeks hurt from how hard I'm grinning, holding on tightly to his arm as we continue strolling to our hotel.

"Should we not wait until the end of the season?"

"Yeah, we will. I just wanted to discuss it with you, see if I should continue doing all that," he replies, kissing the top of my head.

"You should, but I want to help," I say, tilting my head back again.

This time, he kisses me long and hard, and it's the first time in years that he kisses me without anything weighing him down. He kisses me like he's finally breathing properly again. He kisses me like he's ready to start the rest of his life without the anchor pulling him down, holding him back.

He is destined for great things, and he's finally got the time and energy to achieve them all.

Chapter 16

Halo

Making it into the world of Formula One to become a technical director is a hell of a lot harder than I was expecting it to be. I've been applying for low-level engineer positions for over a year now, trying to get one foot in the door, but so far all I've gotten is rejections.

"You're not qualified."

"We have already filled the position."

"We're not looking for people in engineering at the moment."

It's honestly one of the most exhausting things, and even worse, I'm not getting any internships either. So, I'm stuck at this fucking retail job in Moonville, wasting my time somewhere that won't get me to where I want to be.

It makes me worry about the day my sister fights for her spot in F1. With Valentina Romana becoming the first female F1 driver, the chances of my sister getting a spot one day have multiplied by a million, but I don't know if that will be enough for the sport to start inviting more women. She's currently in F4, fighting every single race to work her way into F3 or F2, whichever would be willing to give her a chance.

"Halo, are you okay?" Scarlette asks, and I drape an arm across her shoulders to hug her to my side.

"When have I ever not been?" I challenge with a smirk I don't mean in the slightest.

"Let's see. When Leonard Tick left Grenzenlos you frowned for a week straight and hardly spoke to anyone. When your favorite toothpaste company went out of business and you had to find a new one, you disappeared for three days, not telling anyone where you were going. And a year ago, when you tore your second favorite jacket, you all but had a funeral for it." I step away to give her the shocked look that rant deserves.

"Those were all valid reactions," I reply and point my index finger at her, bringing the sweetest smile to her face.

"I never said they weren't. We were talking about when you weren't okay in the past," she defends with a shrug of her shoulders, but I simply roll my eyes at her before wrapping her in another side hug, this time keeping her there.

A few years ago, around the time I kissed her to make Storm jealous, I realized I could fall for this woman. This ray of sunshine that could turn all of my bad days into good ones. The one that inspired so much joy inside of me. We have a million things in common, and she has the biggest heart of anyone I've ever met. And if she hadn't been so in love with Storm, I could have fallen in love with her. Not in the joking way I always said I was. In the way that I've never *let* myself fall for anyone.

It's a good thing I have full control over my emotions and shut that down before I got my heart broken.

Plus, Scar might just be my best friend in this whole world, even if I'm not hers.

I'm used to being the fun one that never gets asked to stick around. It's why none of my relationships ever worked out and I decided that instead of attempting to find myself a partner that may just leave me when times got tough, I wouldn't try being in a relationship at all.

You can't get your heart broken if you never give it to someone who could trample on it.

Fuck, my thoughts are way too deep today.

I shudder and shake out my limbs, inevitably shaking Scar too. She laughs, a melodic sound that travels through her husband's garage. It calls his attention to her, and he lifts his head from where he's standing next to one of his mechanics who is talking to him about something related to his bike.

"Touching my wife again, Henderson?" he says from all the way across the room without having to raise his voice. The deep sound simply travels through the room effortlessly, the warning as clear in his tone as it is on his features.

"What are you going to do about it?" I challenge because I love fucking with that grumpy man.

Up until he starts storming toward me, which is when I drop my arm and raise my hands in mock surrender. He stops and turns on his heel, not even enjoying getting what he wanted. No. For him it's enough that I'm scared and no longer touching his wife.

"So possessive," I say to Scar and click my tongue, chuckling.

"Yeah, but possessive Julián is sexy. He's always broody, but when it comes to someone being too close to me?" She fans herself with her hand, and I burst into laughter, rolling my lips to hold back more when I see several of the mechanics turn my way. "Oh, also, I should let you know that there will be a Formula 1 driver here later."

My interest is piqued immediately.

"Who?"

"Cameron Kion." My jaw drops all the way to the floor.

"Shut up," I reply, grabbing her arm as if that would tether me to reality because this simply can't be real.

Cameron Kion is my second favorite F1 driver of all time.

He's never won a race before, but he's the fun and easy-going type of person that brings so much light to the sport. No matter what car he's in, he always gives everything he's got. When Adrian Romana went into the sport, he was a hell of a mentor to him. He never speaks badly about the rest of the drivers, instead, he finds a way to joke about the things that clearly piss him off. From what I've heard of him, he also takes care of his family ever since his father abandoned his family, and to top it all of, he was the first F1 driver to come out as gay.

From what Scar has told me, he's not the only queer driver now.

Valentina Romana has told me personally that she's pan, Adrian Romana has flirted more with Storm than his own wife even has, Leonard Tick, although mostly private, has recently shared a lot about being queer in the world of F1 on top of also being the first black driver, and Gabriel Biancheri, according to Scar, very much agrees with his girlfriend that it wouldn't matter to him what gender Valentina identifies as.

He loves her for who she is, not because of her gender.

A man after my own heart.

James Landon, although he hasn't ever discussed his sexuality to me or Scar, gives me the type of vibe that he's very much part of our community as well.

"He'll be here in about half an hour so, please, prepare yourself," Scar says, twisting her arm to get out of my grasp only to put her hand on my arm instead and give it a gentle but warning squeeze.

Okay.

Get my shit together.

I can do that.

Totally.

It's not like I'm about to meet an F1 legend. Someone who's gotten that status simply by having a huge impact on the sport without even winning a race or a championship in his years there.

No.

It'll be fine.

Oh my God, I'm sweating.

The next half hour passes agonizingly slowly, probably because I'm staring at the time on Scar's screen.

But when he finally walks into the room, my breath catches in my throat.

Cameron Kion is about five foot nine, lean but muscular as fuck, especially his thighs, and chiseled beyond anything I've ever seen. He's got curly brown hair and hazel eyes as well as the biggest and brightest smile I've ever seen on a person.

As soon as he approaches, I feel my heart flutter in a way that I don't ever want to fucking dissect because, well, it's never done that before.

I'll simply blame the fact that he's a celebrity.

"Cameron, it's wonderful to see you," Scar says and hugs him, a hug he returns so fully, I'm a little jealous.

I think a hug like that would heal a lot of parts of me that have been broken for far too long.

His gaze shifts to where I'm standing, and he furrows his brows as he studies my expression, the one I currently have no control over.

"Who is pretty boy and why is he looking at me like I'm his savior?" Cameron asks Scar with his thick Australian accent, and a blush immediately heats up my skin. I barely keep the nervous giggle inside because he just called me "pretty boy."

This is not "getting my shit together" at all.

"Cameron, that's Asher 'Halo' Henderson. Halo, this is Cameron," Scar says, turning to me to widen her eyes at me as a way to tell me to unfreeze.

"Nice to meet you, Halo," Cameron says as he extends his hand to me.

"Yeah, nice to meet you, too," I reply and shake his hand, trying not to slap myself for that lame response.

"Is he okay?" Cameron whispers to Scar when I haven't stopped shaking his hand for longer than necessary.

"I'm not sure. He's usually more unaffected and confident than this," Scar whispers back, and I finally manage to release Cameron's hand. A nervous laugh slips past my lips, and I slap a hand in front of my mouth because *what the hell is happening to me?*

Cameron chuckles and places a hand on my shoulder, squeezing it as a way of comfort. What it does is make more embarrassment heat up my cheeks.

Fuck me.

"It's okay to be starstruck. It happened to me the first time I met Fiona Wise." Scar's head snaps toward Cameron at his words.

"No way. You met basketball legend Fiona Wise? In person? No one ever hears anything from her anymore since she's retired."

The two of them fall into a casual conversation about that Fiona lady, and I do my best not to gape at Cameron, but it's so hard not to. On top of being my second favorite F1 driver, he's even better looking in person than he is on a screen, a fact I'm having a very hard time processing at the moment.

Especially because I can't keep from studying his strong, muscular neck, the way his Adam's apple bops as he speaks, and how his full lips shape words.

He has a boyfriend.

He has a boyfriend.

He has a boyfriend.

The mantra is meant to help me stop ogling him, but the only thing that really helps is when Scar tells us the race is starting soon and the three of us turn to her screens as Storm lets his engine roar to life.

It's time for the sighting lap.

CHAPTER 17

Cameron

I've never attended a MotoGP race before. This specific Grand Prix fell on a weekend when I didn't have to race myself and in my home country, so I had to come to see Scarlette and support her and her husband.

We met a year ago during a particularly wild party Leonard Tick hosted to celebrate his wife's gallery opening, her second location in England. He invited Storm and Scarlette, and I spent the night talking to her about Formula One. She wanted to become a race engineer in the sport we both love, and knowing she's finally getting her chance, especially working with one of my favorite people, makes me a very happy man.

She deserves all the success in the world, and if I'd had the power to—meaning I could fire my useless race engineer who hates my guts—I would have hired her on the spot.

"Can I ask you a question?"

A smile tugs at the right side of my mouth.

"Found your voice, have you?" I ask Halo, turning my head to grin at him and find his cheeks still wonderfully red. I don't think that man has stopped blushing since he shook my hand for too long.

"Listen, man, you're super famous, and I admire you a lot, so if I'm a bit awkward, you can only blame yourself," he replies, finally gathering a bit of that confidence Scarlette was talking about before.

"A bit?" I tease him, and he blushes even harder, his face turning an even darker shade of red. "I'm kidding. Ask your question. I'm curious now."

Halo chews on his ridiculously full bottom lip for a second, trying to build up the courage to ask me whatever it is that's weighing on his chest. He's significantly taller than me, so I have to tilt my head back to look into those icy-blue eyes of his. He's also wearing a white polo shirt that complements his tanned skin, and his brown hair sits in messy curls on his head.

"My sister is currently in F4, and she's working her way up into the next categories, but it's really difficult to find sponsors. Do you have any tips or..." Halo trails off, and I cross my arms in front of my chest as I raise my brows at him.

"We know each other for five minutes and you're already asking me for favors?" His eyes widen and his lips part as regret consumes his features.

"No, that's not—I didn't mean—You're just so—" I cut him off.

"I'm messing with you. If we're going to become friends, you're going to have to learn my sense of humor," I say, which seems to settle him a little because his shoulders drop in relief. "What's her name?"

"Nachelle Henderson," he replies and pulls out his phone to show me a picture of her in her racing gear.

"I've heard of her. An up-and-coming driver with a bright future." Halo's eyes soften immensely at my words, and I can tell that he loves his sister. So much so that he'd ask a guy he barely had the confidence to greet for any tips on how to get her further in her career.

It's sweet.

"I'll see if any of my sponsors are looking for new talent to support," I promise him and mean it because F1 is in dire need of more women, and if there is anything I can do to help that happen faster, I will.

Silence stretches between us, and we both shift our attention to the screens again just in time to see Julián leading the rest of the grid into the warm-up lap. He's starting from pole with Viktor right behind him. From what I've gathered from reading up on this season, those two have been fighting each other for first place since the beginning.

Scarlette is working hard, looking at three different screens in front of her at the same time while Storm makes his way across the track, warming his tires.

It's nice to be on this side of it. There is a nervousness weighing on my chest, but it's nothing compared to the one I feel when I'm in the car, getting ready to race.

A lot of people assume that just because it's my job and I do it twenty-plus times a year it would get any easier, but I always get nervous. No matter how long I've been driving, I feel my chest get tight with anticipation and fear.

I'm sure it's the same for Storm, even if he looks calm and collected from this perspective.

The twenty-two riders line up on the grid in their designated spots again, and I find myself holding my breath when all the lights turn on above them.

I wonder if Elijah feels this way before my races, and the thought of my boyfriend has me smiling so hard, my cheeks hurt. I try to get it under control because I notice Halo giving me a confused look, and I don't particularly feel like telling him I'm grinning like an idiot because I've never been this in love before.

Once the lights disappear, Storm and the rest of the riders shoot forward, starting the race. He stays ahead throughout the first three laps, and I find myself relaxing a little when he creates a small gap between himself and Viktor, who seems only too eager to find ways to stick to Storm so he doesn't race away in front.

I'd have expected MotoGP to be a lot more different from Formula One than it actually is.

"Tell me something, Halo. What is it that you do?" I ask when the riders have made their way around the Philip Island Grand Prix Circuit for the fifth time.

"I'm currently working in retail, but it's only until I find a place in F1. I want to become a technical director, so there are a lot of steps I still have to take before I'm even qualified enough to reach that position," he explains, making surprise snake itself around me.

"You're also trying to make it into F1, but you asked me for help for your sister before asking for yourself?" Halo doesn't look at me as I ask the question. He merely shrugs like it's the most natural thing to put others' needs before your own.

"She means more to me than any job in F1 ever would," he says, and I suddenly understand him better than I've ever understood a stranger this quickly.

"I get that. I'd give my life for my siblings. For me, protecting them comes above everything else," I reply and turn my head enough to see him smiling. "What?"

"Nothing. I just wouldn't have expected you to be the one to do the protecting considering you're an F1 driver that puts his life at risk every time he sits in that car. Seems a bit ironic, don't you think?" he asks, so I cross my arms in front of my chest and turn fully to him.

"I do what I do to pay for my siblings to have the best life they could have. I can buy them everything they want and ask for, which isn't a lot because my siblings don't like asking for things. If risking my life means they get to have a good one, then I'll risk my life. Simple as that." Halo nods thoughtfully, clearly agreeing with me.

"So you understand why I asked for my sister and not myself."

It takes everything I've got to fight my smile because I get now what he was trying to do.

"Well played," I say, and Halo grins, winking at me before turning his head back to the screens.

My gaze lingers on him for another long moment, but he doesn't call me out on it. He lets me study him before I turn away, too, focusing entirely on the race.

It's a brutal one.

Storm is fighting Viktor at every turn starting lap seven. They swap positions several times until finally, Viktor makes it stick. He races away, creating a gap of a little over a second over Storm, who is fighting to get back first place.

I'm glued to the screen, chanting for Storm to get Viktor again, but it's not working.

When they cross the line, Storm is in second place. Viktor takes first, closing the gap that the Puerto Rican has done his best to widen, even if it's only by a little.

Scarlette's head drops in defeat, and I know she's as disappointed as her husband is right now.

As disappointed as I am most days when I cross the finish line not a winner.

It's a pain that never gets easier.

Chapter 18

Julián

After coming in second place in Australia, I went on to come in fourth in Malaysia. The only reason I wasn't upset about that loss was because the Prima Pantera riders came first and second and one of the Saturn Racing riders came in third, which means fourth wasn't a bad way to finish to keep my first place in the standings. I even gained three points because Viktor came sixth.

It's fair to say that we were both struggling on that track.

There are two races left in the season, and I've got a big enough lead that if I win in Portugal, I could win the championship if Viktor finishes anywhere below third place. Since that isn't likely to happen, though, I'll have to wait until we're racing in Valencia to snatch my first championship title.

Fuck, Scar's positivity is rubbing off on me if I'm already so certain I'll be World Champion.

I wander through our house, not entirely sure what to do with myself. Before the board sold my father's company and bought me out, I spent all of my free time answering emails, attending meetings, online and in person, and calling people to check in with them. Now? Now, I don't have to do any of that.

All I have to do is rest, and I'm having a hard time sitting still.

"*Arcoíris, ¿dónde estás?*" I call through our house, Jax on my heels. He doesn't often leave my side, just like Diablo doesn't leave Scar's.

Silence follows my question, and worry settles deep within my chest.

There are exactly four reasons why Scar wouldn't answer me.

1. She didn't hear me.

2. She's listening to music through her headphones and *can't* hear me.

3. She's sleeping.

4. She's having anxiety and is hiding from the world.

Over the years, it's almost like I've developed a sixth sense, telling me exactly which of the four is happening. It's why I know Scar is having anxiety right now.

I find her sitting on our bed with my small blanket, the one I keep because I get cold very easily, wrapped around her. My wife is staring absentmindedly at the show that's playing on the television. It's one of her comfort ones, the ones she rewatches over and over because her anxiety isn't too great with trying to watch new things.

"Why didn't you come to me?" I ask as I approach our bed. Diablo is on his blanket at the foot of the bed, and he barely lifts his head to acknowledge me. Jax jumps onto the bed as well, curling up against Diablo.

"It's not that bad. It's just—" She cuts off and places her hand on her chest. "It's sitting right here. No trigger. No logical reason. It's simply there," she explains as I settle down beside her on the mattress.

"You could have still gotten me. I would have replaced that blanket so you could smell me directly," I say because I see the way she's wrapped it around herself and brought it as close to her nose as possible.

My scent seems to have a similar calming effect as lavender does for her.

"I didn't want to bother you," she explains, her blue eyes red from exhaustion. The circles underneath her eyes tell me a million things she does her best to hide.

Things she eventually always shares with me because she feels safe with me.

"Love, you are never, ever a bother. You know that. You're my top priority." I lift my hand to her cheek to wipe away the single tear that escaped her left eye.

"Then distract me so I don't focus on this feeling inside my chest. Please," she says, her voice soft and careful to make sure I know she's not demanding anything of me.

She's simply asking for help.

"What do you need? Cuddles? Food? Go for a ride? One or several orgasms?" Any of these suggestions have helped her in the past, and as much as I know her better than I know myself most of the time, it depends on how bad her anxiety is. So, I need her to tell me which of these things would help her the most.

"Can we go for a bike ride?" she asks, and I lean forward to kiss her as I slowly remove my blanket from her body. Scar smiles against my mouth, letting it fall from her shoulders as she wraps her arms around me, deepening the kiss.

"We can go for a bike ride first, then we'll see how you feel about the other options," I say and do my best not to keep kissing her because that would only lead to me kissing her somewhere much lower, and she asked to go for a bike ride.

Not for the orgasms.

"Fine," she says and pouts playfully like I'm the one who made the decision.

"Come on, Scar." I get off the bed and hold my hand out for her. She slips her palm against mine, allowing me to help her up. There's already more calmness inside of her, the kind she usually gets when she's around me for a while, and it warms my chest to see how much she depends on me too.

Because I depend on her a lot.

In a healthy relationship, there has to be a balance between needing your partner, wanting them, depending on them, and giving them space, something I think Scar and I have perfected over the years.

"Thank you for coming to check on me," she says as we make our way down the stairs and toward our garage where our bikes are.

"Next time, I need you to come to me, Scar, unless you need a second alone. Staying away because you feel like a bother is a firm no. You come to me when you need me. End of discussion." She chuckles softly, a sound that travels through me, leaving the most wonderful sensation behind.

My entire body feels like it softens as the tension leaves it.

"Yes, sir."

The tension returns tenfold, but only in the lower half of my body.

Puñeta, esa mujer me tiene loco...

It's always so peaceful when Scar and I go for a ride. Today, because of her anxiety, she's backpacking, and I'd be lying if I said I didn't prefer it when she rides with me. There are so many assholes on the road, and this way I feel like I can protect her best.

Plus, the way she touches me when she's riding backpack?

It's my weakness.

We're speeding down the highway for a while, both of us in the mood for some zoomies. The wind is coming at us from the front at such a speed that it feels significantly more difficult to go for zoomies, but luckily, my bike has enough horsepower to still let us race down the highway.

We may not be going the speed limit exactly, but there's hardly anyone on the road at this time. The occasional car we pass gives us a thumbs up or greets us in a way that lets me know they're also bikers.

We're free when we're out here. Free from the weight of the championship. Free from our grief and trauma. Free from anything and everything that tries to hurt us.

Eventually, after what feels like an eternity and not nearly long enough, I pull off the highway again so we can make our way home.

"How are you feeling?" I ask when we reach a stoplight, letting go of my handlebars to rub her knees. We have motorcycle comms in, so she can hear me easily and I can hear her as well.

"Much, much better," she says as she rubs her hands down my stomach and then my thighs.

There's not a single car beside us when I say, "Yeah? Then show me."

I don't have to elaborate. Scar knows exactly what I mean as she trails her hands onto my stomach again before dropping one of them between my legs to cup my already aching cock through my motorcycle gear. A gear I regret putting on almost immediately because I can hardly feel her, and my dick is begging for more contact.

"Hurry home, husband, so I can touch you properly," Scar says, rubbing her hand over my hard bulge twice more before removing it. I groan, knowing the sound will go straight into her ears, and she lets out a little whimper that has me racing down the main street toward our house.

Once we're inside our garage, I lower the doors again at the same time as I turn off my bike and put it on its kickstand.

I jump off the bike, but Scar stays on it, flinging one of her legs to the other side so she's facing me while still remaining on the seat. She only moves enough to go on the spot I just occupied. Her helmet is covering her face, so I can't see her expression well enough to read her intention there.

"On the bike?" I ask while already removing my jacket.

"Why are my pants still on?" is Scar's only response right as I rip my shirt off, not even bothering to take my helmet off.

"*¿Qué quieres, mami?* Hmm?" I say as I close the distance between us. "Want me to take our helmets off and slowly undress you? Or keep them on, remove only the bare minimum, and fuck you so hard, we'll have to stay in bed for the next few days to recover?" My hand lifts to her helmet, grabbing the underside of it to bring her face closer to mine. I snap up her visor to reveal her blue eyes are filled with lust.

"I want it hard and fast. I want you to leave your helmet on but lift your visor too so I can look into your beautiful eyes while you fuck away my ability to walk for a few days. I want what you want."

Scar lifts my visor before running her hand down my naked chest, rubbing her thumbs over my nipples and sending a wave of pleasure down my spine, straight to my cock. I'm aching, and she knows it. She's playing with me.

"Ass up. Let me take off your pants," I instruct, watching my wife obey quickly. I undo the button of her leathers and pull down her pants, slipping her underwear down at the same time. I drag her to the edge of the seat and unzip my pants just enough to take my cock out.

"Oh yes," my wife says, and I look up at her to see her attention is on my dick.

Fuck.

Me.

She watches the whole time as I bring the head of it to her entrance, pushing it inside of her just enough to coat it in her arousal.

"Stop teasing. Give me all of it," she demands, and it's her sexy-as-hell bossy tone that has me driving inside of her without another moment of hesitation. Scar is so turned on, I slip inside with ease, and we both moan at the feel of her walls wrapping around me.

Heaven.

Paradise.

Home.

All words that fit only too well when Scar and I are connected like this, without anything between us anymore.

Except, she's still wearing too many clothes.

I drag down the zipper of her jacket and push it down her shoulders so I can lift her shirt up and cup her beautiful breast.

"No bra, love?" I ask, bringing a smile to her lips.

"You know I hate those things."

Oh yes, I do.

We've made a lot of unforgettable memories because of it.

I slip out of her and thrust back in, hard and fast as she commanded. My hand on her breast tightens its grip as my thumb and index finger pinch her nipple. Scar's hand lifts to my nape where she holds on as I fuck her harder and faster with every stroke.

"Oh fuck," I moan as she screams my name, her eyes pressing shut. Her nails dig into my nape, deeper and deeper as I keep driving into her with so much force, the whole bike shakes.

Our skin slapping against each other is the only sound filling our garage apart from our moans, and it only drives my pleasure higher until I can't hold back anymore.

I moan and groan, my entire body on fire with desire. Both of my hands drop to her naked ass, and I hold on tight as I go faster, chasing our orgasms because there is no way in hell I'll last when Scar's breasts are bouncing with every thrust. When she keeps her eyes on me the entire time. When she's pricking me with her nails, the combination of pain and pleasure bringing me even closer to my release.

"I'm so close. Oh my God, I'm gonna come," she says, cupping her own breast to pinch her nipple.

Part of me wishes I'd taken my helmet off so I could pull it into my mouth, but I know my wife has a little bit of a mask kink, and I'm very on board with that kink. I'll wear whatever mask she wants me to.

We did have a lot of fun on Halloween last year when I was dressed up as Simon "Ghost" Riley.

"Hold on tight," I say as I lift her left ass cheek a little, angling her in a way that makes sure I hit that perfect spot that always makes her fall apart quickly.

With every thrust, I rub against it. With every thrust, she cries louder until she finally shakes in my arms, her fingernails digging into my back and slowly dragging down. She's marking me, and the thought of that alone is enough to make my next thrust be my final one before my orgasm takes over.

It's so strong that I can't do anything but hold onto her and let it wash through me in waves.

It doesn't stop for a long time, especially when Scar wraps her legs around me, digging her heels into my ass. I run my hands over her thick thighs, loving the way they're trembling.

But not quite enough yet.

"Can you stand?" I ask, nudging her helmet with mine.

"Probably, why?" Her laugh is carefree and breathless, happiness spreading through my chest at the sound.

"Then we're not done yet."

Chapter 19

Julián

Viktor only qualified seventh yesterday while I got pole.

We're in Portugal at the Algarve International Circuit.

The second to last race of the season.

If we finish in these positions, I'll win. I'll win my first championship, and it won't be to save my father's company.

It'll be for me.

For Scar.

For our dreams.

We will make a name for ourselves in the world of motorsport, and even though she's going to go work with Valentina next year, we will have this forever. We will be written into history together.

The thought has me smiling under my helmet while I wait for the green light to take the sighting lap. I lift my visor as I sit on my bike, looking over at where Scar is doing a million things. She catches me staring at her, a blush covering her cheeks as a small smile pulls up the corners of her mouth. It turns into a full-faced smile when I wink at her, shut my visor, and then shoot out of the garage as soon as I'm given the green light.

I'm the first one to make my way down the pitlane, on my way to go a lap around the track and find my spot on the grid. It's only sixty degrees outside, which is a nice change from the races when it's ninety or higher and I sweat my ass off during the sighting and warm-up laps.

In corner three, I feel my bike shuddering a little, as if something isn't quite right with the engine.

"What the fuck?" After the corner, I right my bike again, going down the straight slower than normally.

Then my worst nightmare happens.

The engine cuts out.

My bike keeps going, but only because of the momentum.

But soon, it stops altogether, and I barely have enough time and strength to keep it upright as I guide it toward one of the access areas on the track where the marshals come out to take care of a bike that breaks down.

"Fuck, fuck, fuck," I curse over and over, dropping my bike near the marshals and yelling an apology to the ones that are going to have to take care of it while I run.

There is another marshal already waiting for me on a little moped, ready to take me back to the pits.

"As fast as you can, please," I call out because there is a fifteen-minute window between when the pitlane opens for us riders to take our sighting lap and when it closes again so no one can get out.

If I don't make it back in time, I'm not starting the race.

My heart is racing uncontrollably. Fear has infiltrated every part of my body. I could lose the championship all because my bike gave up on me.

It wouldn't even be a fault on my end.

It wouldn't be Scar's fault either, but I know she'd blame herself regardless.

"Please hurry," I tell the marshal, squeezing his shoulder. He picks up speed, and I thank him three times.

I can't let my wife blame herself for this.

We make it with exactly three minutes to spare. I'm running through the pitlane, noting that all the other riders have already left and made their way onto the grid. My lungs are burning from panic and the running as I sprint all the way to my garage where my crew is already waiting for another bike.

The clock on the left side is taunting me.

Two minutes.

I don't waste any time. I simply fling my leg over the machine, grab hold of the handlebars, then speed down the pitlane just shy of going too fast, which would earn me a penalty.

The clock reads one minute when I make it out of the pitlane, and once I'm on the track, I let out a sigh of relief.

That was way too fucking close.

And the worst part of it all is that the sighting lap isn't even the hardest part of race day.

No.

The race is, and we have yet to even complete one racing lap.

If the day continues the way it has started, then I'm not winning shit today.

Twenty-five laps.

This race is twenty-five laps long, and while that may not seem like much, it's currently the only thing standing between me and the championship, apart from Viktor.

The warm-up lap does fuck all to calm my nerves, but at least it allows me to enter my zone. The crowd may be screaming and cheering, but I drown them out. I have to. There's only one goal, only one thing I have to focus on, and that is winning.

Winning this race.

Winning the championship.

Okay, part of me also hopes Viktor stays fourth or lower, but that is only happening in the back of my mind.

Where he finishes can't be a priority for me at the moment. It'll only distract me, and I can't have that. Whether he finishes second or third is irrelevant if it leads me to make a mistake that costs me the win.

If I win, the chances of me taking the championship increase exponentially, even if Viktor finishes high enough to prevent me from taking the title today.

In moments like these, I wish there was some communication between Scar and me. The silence, apart from the muffled sounds of bike engines and cheering fans, is putting a heavy weight on my chest that's making it harder and harder to breathe. There may no longer be the fate of a company resting on my shoulders, but failure still isn't something I enjoy experiencing. It's why my whole body revolts against the mere possibility of it.

Once we're back at the starting grid, it's only a matter of seconds until the lights turn out, telling us to get ready for the start of the race. I look in my mirrors to see the safety car and the rest of the grid with either one leg touching the ground or both. I only ever use one leg while waiting for the race to start.

Once the lights turn off, I shoot forward, my reaction time not fast enough to keep both Prima Pantera riders behind me.

Joseph overtakes me.

We move into the first corner and lean down at almost the same time. My leg is extended in the way it always is before we get back to a straight and I right my bike, tucking in my leg again.

I stay right behind Joseph, going into the next corner with our wheels almost touching. He's a great defender, though, which means he keeps the first-place spot as he shoots forward again and I chase after him.

It may not be as hot here as it has been on the other tracks I've been to this season, but that doesn't stop sweat from collecting at my nape and dripping down my back with every lap I fight to get back ahead.

The screens on the side of the track tell me that Viktor lost three places during the start, a good sign for me. Except, he is a fantastic rider, and he will get back into the top places if the rest of the riders don't make it extra difficult for him to do so.

The only reason why the smallest bit of hope enters my chest is because Tanner is in ninth, and Tanner fucking hates Viktor's guts.

He will hold him up for as long as he can.

The laps fly past.

Joseph and I have created a bit of distance between ourselves and the rest of the grid, but I'm still right behind him at less than zero-point-three seconds.

We're halfway through the race when I finally overtake him again in the last corner, and I use the momentum of going into it a little faster than I should have as I right my bike once more to speed down the track faster than he is.

I make the overtake stick.

But he continues to fight me, staying within zero-point-two seconds of me the entire time I look at the screens on the side of the track or my dashboard.

And those screens are also showing that Viktor is up in sixth place now.

Three more, and I'm fucked.

There are ten laps left.

The crowds are cheering for me every time I pass by the grandstands that are occupied by fans. They believe in me to bring this home. I saw all of their posters during the Rider Fan Parade. They have so much faith in me, and I hope to all that is good in the world that it isn't misplaced.

That I'm deserving of them.

Nine laps left.

Part of me tries to see Scar every time that I down the straight where the start and finish line is. She keeps sending me messages on my dashboard, but they're only the pre-approved ones she's allowed to send me. There is nothing personal about them, nothing to encourage me and tell me to keep doing what I'm doing and that I'll win if I do. One look at her face where she's sitting at the pitwall would be enough for me, but I can't see her.

Eight laps left.

Joseph is still right behind me. Every corner I take, he takes it with me. Every time I think I'm creating more of a distance between us, he closes it again. Every move I make, he's there, matching it effortlessly on his Prima Pantera.

Seven laps left.

Kwan is catching up to his teammate and me. I'm still keeping track of the gaps, and every time I race by a screen, it shows him catching up.

Six laps left.

My tires are starting to lose grip. I have medium tires for both tires this time, and as long as they have lasted already, they're starting to feel like they're degrading more and more quickly by the second.

Four laps left.

I think I've started holding my breath at some point, and my lungs burn in protest at the exhaustion and lack of oxygen combination.

Three laps left.

Every time I lean down to take a corner, trying to perfectly balance going low but not too low so that my knee touches the ground fully and it causes me to crash out of the race. It's a fickle thing, and I'm getting more scared with every dip in the corner that I'll lose it so close to the end.

Two laps left.

The screen at the side of the track near the finish line says that Viktor has only made his way into fifth place.

One lap left.

Victory is at the tip of my fingers.

I'm three corners into the lap when my bike suddenly makes the same weird noise my other one made right before the engine died out.

My heart drops into my stomach.

"Please, don't do this to me," I say to the bike as if it could understand me.

It makes the same noise again, and I'm giving everything I have to get through this lap as fast as possible.

I'm not giving up when I'm this close to winning.

The noise continues, and I feel something inside the bike rumbling, but I ignore it as I push forward. I ignore Scar's messages on the dashboard too. I don't want to know what's wrong.

I just need to make it three more corners.

Two more.

One more.

My engine shuts off right as I go down the straight, but I have enough momentum to keep going.

Enough of a gap so that when I roll over the finish line, I'm still in first.

All of my fans explode into celebrations before they have to watch me not so gently crash my bike into the gravel. The first time it happened to me today, I somehow managed to guide it to a stop. Not this time. This time is clumsy. And not at all graceful.

A gasp leaves every fan where I'm crashing the bike, and this time, I don't get up. There's no more pressure to.

I've won.

I've done it.

The title is mine, and I get to enjoy it now with my wife.

My wife.

A surge of adrenaline hits me. Scar is waiting for me, and I have to get to her.

A hand appears in front of my face, and it taps against my visor. I tilt my head to see Tanner holding out his other hand to help me up. There are marshals picking up my bike and coming to check on me too, but I ignore them and place my gloved hand in Tanner's. He helps me up, and I give him a brief hug as he congratulates me on winning.

Then, I'm running.

I'm using every bit of adrenaline I have left to get to Scar, and she's already waiting for me when I enter the pitlane and get to the first, second, and third place sign. My team is standing behind her, waiting for me, too, and I let the tears fall as I race to pull my wife into my arms. She was expecting me, but I have to hold onto her a little tighter to keep both of us from falling because of the impact of my hug.

Scar is laughing and crying as she hugs me back.

"*Tú ganaste, mi amor*," she says and pulls back to press a kiss to my helmet where my mouth would be if I wasn't wearing it. I grab her face and look into her blue eyes as more tears fall down my cheek.

"*No, arcoíris.* Nosotros *ganamos*." Because without her strategies, without her keeping everything under control for me from her side, we wouldn't be here.

"Yes, we did." She jumps up and down first, and I join her a moment before the rest of my team approaches us and wraps us in a big hug.

I've never been this happy.

And I hope that wherever my father is, he's proud of me too.

14
14
14

Epilogue

Scarlette

Over A Year Later

"As much as I loved living in Moonville, it has *nothing* on living in Monaco," I tell my husband, who is currently lounging on his chair on our veranda.

Julián let me convince him that we should use the money we got through the buy-out to get ourselves a house in Monaco with a pool because our babies love swimming, especially Jax. The second we moved in and he saw the pool, he jumped into it, and I have never seen our seven-year-old so excited. Naturally, Julián panicked and jumped in right after him, but he swam away from him the entire time, not ready to leave the water. After the initial shock, it was a little funny to me.

Not to my grump, though.

"Well, I fucking hated living in Moonville, so I would agree." I chuckle at his dry comment, and he tilts his head to smile my way.

Jax is curled up at his feet, the huge Berner having pushed Julián's legs apart to make space for himself. Diablo tried to go between mine as well, but he's too big for the chair, so he went to lie beside me. They're both wet from going swimming a little while ago, their fur only slowly drying because of how thick it is.

"I think we made the right decision moving here," I add, and there is something in my voice that has him standing up and walking toward me. Jax takes advantage of him leaving and falls on his side, taking up even more space on the chair.

Meanwhile, Julián makes his way onto *my* chair, rearranging us until we both fit on it, me between his legs with his arms around me and my head on his chest. He kisses the top of my head, then my temple as we both enjoy the warm temperature.

"We did, love. We made the right choice."

His scent envelops me, and a sense of calm infiltrates my system until I feel my eyes fluttering shut.

My first year as Valentina Romana's race engineer went by amazingly. We won her home Grand Prix, and the rest of her races, for the most part, went so well, she even got the Rookie of the Year award recently.

We had a good year.

Elias is still part of Julián's father's company, but he's been demoted and has significantly less work. According to him, he doesn't mind that as much now that they have Liliana because it means he gets to spend more time with his daughter. However, that also means they couldn't move to Monaco with us even though we were planning to move somewhere together.

"The only downside is having to see Adrian's smug face a lot more often," Julián says after a while, and I burst out laughing.

"Please, you love him. And you also love Leonard, Chiara, Leonora, Cameron, Val, Gabriel, Nevaeh, James and his kid Damian. Their little family has taken us in, and you adore them all."

He doesn't argue with me because he knows it would be pointless.

He knows I'm right.

"Whatever. If someone asked me what I needed in life, it wouldn't be their names I'd speak. It would be yours," he says and tilts my head up by my chin, kissing my lips. "And theirs," he adds and uses his chin to point toward Jax and Diablo.

"I feel the same," I reply, raising my hand to place it on his cheek. I trace his birthmark there while I study his differently-colored eyes with a grin on my face. "Well, and our bikes."

That brings a big smile to his face.

"Of course. We can't forget about our bikes," he says and kisses me again, this time until we're both breathless and have to come up for air.

"I love you, my Storm."

"*Te quiero mucho, mi arcoíris.*"

The End

Wondering what the other Pitstop Series characters are up to?

Here is a compilation of short stories to answer your questions.

Make sure you read all books in *The Pitstop Series* up until and including *Straight To The Chapel* to avoid any spoilers.

Nevaeh Has A Surprise For Adrian

Adrian

My wife has a surprise for me.

I've been kicking my feet all day like an idiot because the last time she said she had a surprise for me, she told me she was ready for us to try having a baby. She went all Deadpool—one of our favorite Marvel movies—and held up a box with her IUD. Then, she lifted her dress over her head to reveal an orange lingerie set that barely covered her body.

And, well, I don't think I have to tell any of you why that was one of the best nights of my life.

"I don't even care where you're taking me as long as it is to Nevaeh," I tell my sister, who has been suspiciously quiet all morning.

We're supposed to have one of our sibling days when it's just the two of us hanging out, but since she picked me up from home, I knew something was different.

She's in on Nevaeh's surprise.

"Why would I be taking you to see Nevaeh?" she asks as she pulls onto the highway, the same route we take when we go to her academy. Which is where she told me we'd be going, but I still don't trust that she doesn't know anything and/or isn't in on the surprise, too.

"Because she said she has a surprise for me, and you've been acting weird for the past three hours," I reply, and she throws me an offended look.

"I haven't been acting weird! I just spent the last three hours having brunch with you and talking non-stop about what's going on in my life. How is that weird?" She's focusing on the road, so she can't see my "I'm not buying your bullshit" face.

So, I wait until she turns my way, and as soon as she catches a glimpse of my expression, she starts smiling in a way that tells me she *does* know something and I am *not* reading into things. It's honestly my favorite thing because it means I'm right.

"Can you just shut up and drop it?" she asks and punches me in the arm.

"Ow, what the hell was that for?" I rub the sore spot.

"Call it sisterly annoyance because my older brother made me give him my tell that I know stuff he's not supposed to know." I snicker in my seat and roll my lips to keep my mouth shut. My arm still hurts, and I don't want to earn another punch to it.

Part of me was hoping to see Nevaeh standing outside the academy, but she isn't. I'm still convinced I'm right, though, so I wait patiently for Val to lead me inside the karting track building I've been to endless times.

"Can you carry something to my office?" Val asks as she leads me through the whole building, Nevaeh nowhere to be found.

"What the hell? Where is she?" I ask and turn to Val to see her picking up a bag of soccer balls.

"Where is who?"

If I wouldn't rip out my own heart before I let anything happen to Val, I'd strangle her.

"My wife."

I try to keep the irritation out of my voice, but it's difficult.

I don't like to be kept from Nevaeh.

"She's at home, waiting for you while doing some important journalism stuff," Val replies but doesn't look at me.

"'Journalism stuff' meaning..." I trail off, waiting for her to fill in the blanks because who the fuck uses those words to describe what their best friend does?

The answer is: not my sister.

"Just tell me what's going on," I plead.

"No," is her only response before she points at the bag full of basketballs, signaling for me to pick them up.

You would tell me what's happening if you knew, right?

We spend the next two hours doing chores around the academy. Since it's closed today and there are no private lessons either, Val is using the opportunity to do some maintenance. The only problem is that she's making me do all the hard work, and by the time she tells me to take a break, sweat is dripping down my back.

"This is my least favorite way to spend time together," I say as I drop into the seat in her office, grabbing her water bottle off the desk to gulp down the whole thing.

"Think of all the kids that are benefitting from you doing things like filling the soccer balls with air, restocking the first-aid kit, and everything else I've had you do today. You're preparing to be a father, so it's good that you know how to do all of this stuff," she argues, and damn her, it's too valid a point to keep complaining.

"Fine. What else do you need me to do now?"

Val shuffles her papers around before landing on a to-do list she obviously created for me. She checks off all the tasks I've completed while I frown at her because now I'm a little annoyed.

"You know you could have hired someone to do all of this. We're millionaires," I remind her, but she gives me the unimpressed look that statement deserves.

"When your child's favorite kart needs to be oiled, are you going to call someone to do it for you? Or are you going to do it yourself and teach your kid in the process for some nice bonding time?"

"I guess I'm going to go oil the karts," I say, which earns me the brightest smile from my sister. "I feel like I've been played."

"You may have been, but hey, I'm going to milk that whole you wanting to be a good dad thing for as long as I can," she says with a little chuckle, and I lift my pinky into the air, flipping her off in the way that is so personal to our family. "Love you, too," she calls after me, but I shake my head as I walk away.

I may be smiling, but deep inside, I'm annoyed.

Definitely not amused.

No way.

My feet bring me toward where the karts are when I finally see her.

Mon ange.

Mon paradis.

My Nevaeh.

She's standing at the barrier of the karting track in the same orange dress she wore all those years ago to the club where we first got closer. When I first touched her in ways I never thought I'd be allowed to touch her. The night I realized I hadn't wanted anyone since I met her. The night I realized I'd never want anyone else ever again.

"I've been waiting for you to show up all day," I admit as I stalk toward her, watching a brilliant smile take over her face.

"Is that so?" she asks with a playful gleam in her eyes, one I long to see every day because it makes me so happy when she's this way.

"Yup. Was going out of my mind not being near you, if I'm being honest." When I reach her, I place both of my hands on her hips, noticing that she's hiding her hands behind her back. I try to look around her, but she moves her head to block my view.

"You saw me this morning. And had me naked and wrapped around you all night."

"It's never enough." I kiss her, the insatiable side of me taking over because I meant what I said.

It's never enough.

No matter how often I kiss her, touch her, smell her, it's not enough. There's a constant need inside of me to get more, and Nevaeh seems to feel the same because she kisses me back even harder, slipping her tongue into my mouth.

And as much as I want to lose myself in the kiss, I'm also very curious to know what she's hiding from me.

I slip my hands from her hips and onto her wrists, but she catches onto what I'm doing quickly and breaks the kiss to take a step back.

"Nice try," she says, still carrying that smile on her now reddened lips.

"I'm an impatient man, Nevaeh. Show me what you're hiding. I need to know what the surprise is," I beg, the distance between us making me step toward her a little. She tilts her head back to look up at me, her hands remaining behind her back.

"You're going to have to learn to be patient because this surprise is going to take a while to grow," she says right before bringing what she was hiding to the front.

In the palm of her hand rests a replica of my helmet, except it's hardly big enough to fit a baby's head.

Oh my God.

"Nevaeh—" I start but cut off because a wave of emotion hits me right in the chest when I see the tears collecting in her eyes.

"Thank God you got it. I was scared you would think the surprise is me simply getting you a tiny version of your helmet," she says, and I'd be offended that she thinks I'm so oblivious if it wasn't totally a possibility.

"You're pregnant." I have to say the words out loud to believe them. If I don't, then it all remains a fantasy that can't quite sink in.

"I am. We're going to have a baby," she says and places the tiny helmet on the karting track barrier so she can grab my face in both of her hands, wiping away my tears as they fall.

"I never thought I'd get this," I whisper, my feelings so overwhelming, I silently gasp for breath because I'm having a hard time remembering I need oxygen. "I never thought I'd find you," I add because even after all this time, it feels surreal to me to be married to the love of my life, the other half of my soul.

"But you did. You found me taking pictures of your rental car, and you thought, being the arrogant ass that you are, that I was taking pictures of you. Now that's a story you can tell our child when they're old enough to understand it," she says, still rubbing my cheeks and catching the tears I have no control over.

They keep flowing down without the ability to be held back. They drop as if they had to, almost like taking a breath and expelling it.

"Yeah, but when I tell our child that story, I'm going to tell them you *were* taking pictures of me and not the car." Nevaeh starts giggling as I bring my hands back to her hips, this time dragging her against my chest.

"Of course you are," she says and rolls her eyes playfully. "As long as you tell them that I took the best pictures of you that you'd ever seen."

"Naturally," I reply, my hands dropping to her stomach. "You're pregnant." I should probably stop repeating my words like a broken record player, but I'm still too stuck in disbelief to process what's happening.

We haven't been trying for that long.

"As pregnant as I was twenty seconds ago, yup," she says and giggles all over again.

I grab her chin between my thumb and index finger like I always do before leaning down to press my lips to hers. Her giggle continues to make her chest shake, and I smile against her mouth because of how sweet she is.

"You're making all of my dreams come true, *mon paradis*," I admit as I place my forehead against hers, my tears finally slowing.

"And you mine, *mein Mond*."

My arms wrap around her in a firm bear hug, and I don't let her go for a long time. I cup the back of her head and hold onto her like my life depends on it because she's the only thing tethering me to reality at the moment.

We're going to have a baby.

I'm going to be a dad.

I don't know whether to panic, throw up, or dance around in joy. Perhaps a combination of all three things would be the right way to react to news like this, but holding Nevaeh is a lot better than doing any of that.

"I love you so much," I tell her, kissing her temple, cheek, and lips until she's laughing the kind of laugh that makes me weak in the knees.

"I love you, Adrian." She steps on her tiptoes to kiss me more deeply, and I lose myself entirely in her this time.

My hand rubs over her stomach as if I could make sure it protects our baby as well as Nevaeh.

Breaking the kiss, I go back to placing my forehead against Nevaeh's, breathing in her scent.

"This is the best surprise I've ever gotten."

Valentina Wins Her First Championship

Valentina

James crashes out of the race.

My rival, the only thing standing in my way to take this championship title, hits the wall on the last lap of the Grand Prix.

My heart stops beating for a second before I shake my head and refocus on the track.

I haven't won yet. I still have to bring my car all the way to the finish line.

"Scarlette," I say as I push my radio button. I don't need to say anything else. She knows me well enough to know exactly what I need to hear from her.

"He's okay."

Relief washes through me, and I would exhale in the next corner if the G-force didn't hit my body as hard as it does.

Holding my breath, I push through it.

Sweat drips down my forehead and back. Abu Dhabi at this time of the year is still fucking hot, especially today. It's almost thirty degrees, and it feels like my body has slowly been cooking in my seat for the last hour. My skin is burning, my body totally and utterly exhausted.

Scar told me that one of the Klein drivers had to retire from the heat, and I can't blame him even in the slightest.

If I was still in one of the mid- or low-field teams, if my championship wasn't on the line, I'd have asked to retire as well.

Okay, that's a lie.

I'm too stubborn to do that, but it's something I definitely should have done in that situation, so I'm proud of him for knowing his limits.

"Almost there," Scarlette tells me when I've made my way halfway across the track.

"I'm dying," I reply, which is perhaps Adrian-level dramatic, but it's also the only way to describe how I'm feeling right now.

"Copy. You're not the only one. Adrian was on the radio saying he's not having fun being barbecued." I can't help but chuckle because I guess I'm not as dramatic as Adrian after all.

The last few corners feel like hell and this lap feels like the longest lap of the entire race, even though I know it isn't.

But I can't believe how close I am to achieving something no woman before me has ever been given the opportunity to achieve.

And when I cross the finish line and fireworks created by drones light up the sky, I have officially proved every single asshole who ever doubted me wrong.

Every person who has stood in the way of accomplishing my dream.

Every man who told me women do not belong in motorsport because they're not capable enough.

I'm officially living proof that women can become Formula One world champions, and I hope with every fiber of my being that that is enough to finally make everyone else, all of the teams, open their doors to more women.

I hope all of my struggles to get to where I am will mean more than just me winning a championship.

I hope they will be enough reason for more change to take root in the sport I have loved since I was a child.

The cool-down lap allows me to take deep breaths, the overwhelming feelings inside of me keeping me from even crying because I finally did it.

Gabriel's words are ringing in my ears.

You're Valentina Romana, future Formula One champion.

Now I'm Valentina Romana, *current* Formula One champion.

As soon as I've driven my car to the first place sign, the tears finally drop down my cheeks and I simply sit there while every single one of my fans cheers for me. My Velocità Rossa is still hot from the high track temperature, so I can't go out and hug it to thank it for bringing me to where I am right now. That's why I stay in the car, barely lifting my visor enough to bring my gloved fingers to my eyes and wipe away my tears.

It's only when Adrian's hand appears inside my car and pulls out my steering wheel that I snap out of my trance of overwhelmed emotions. He places it on top of my car and brings his hand to my halo, leaning down and into my car with his helmet-covered head.

"Are you okay?" he asks, loud enough so I can hear him through the padding of two helmets.

"I can't feel my legs," I admit, my hands shaking now because of the exhaustion and amount of joy hitting my body, it doesn't know what to do with all of the feelings inside of me.

"That's okay. Take your time, then get out of your car and celebrate this win with your team. With your husband. With me," he says and pats the top of my helmet.

Without Adrian, I wouldn't be here. He fought every step of the way to get me here, fought the people who were in my way with me, and I wish I could get out of the car and hug him, telling him how thankful I am that he never gave up on me.

Even when I gave up on myself.

It takes me another moment to gather up the strength to get out of the car. I use my halo to jump out, my legs almost giving in. Luckily, Adrian didn't go far, and he hugs me to cover up my weak legs.

"Dad and Grandfather would be so, so proud of you if they were here, Val. You achieved everything they hoped you would and more," my brother says, and I start sobbing in his arms because I wish they were here. I'm glad he is here. I wish I wouldn't have taken this title from my best friend to get it, but it's exactly what he would have done if it was the other way around. That's a Formula One driver's way, and that's exactly who I am.

"Thank you for holding me upright," I say once I stop sobbing, which happens quickly because I don't want any of the reporters or fans of other drivers, or doubters for that matter, to criticize me for crying as much as I am.

They'll only blame it on me being a woman, not on the months I've been fighting for this title, on the years it took me to get here.

They'll call me hormonal.

They've done so in the past, and they will do it again if I don't get a grip on my emotions.

"I love you," I tell my brother right before I let go of him.

A second later, my favorite pair of arms in the world wrap around me, lifting me off the ground. He drops me quickly so I can spin in his arms to see he has taken off his helmet and tears are streaming down his face. He grabs my helmet on both sides and shakes my head as he lets out a victorious scream that has me grinning and crying all over again. Then I'm screaming with him before we both jump on the spot. He wraps me up in his arms again, and I wish the helmet away so I could feel my husband's lips on mine during one of the most special moments of my career.

"You won, mon tournesol. You are the champion. *You*." The way he emphasizes the last word has me smiling even harder.

"I beat nineteen other drivers fair and square," I reply with a happy lilt in my voice.

"You did. You beat our asses, just like I always knew you would," Gabriel says right after leaning back again to kiss my helmet. He's obviously as impatient to kiss me as I am him, but he will have to wait a second longer.

I've got a team to celebrate with.

"Go," he says without me having to say a single word, and I waste no time sprinting toward where my team is standing, including Lorenzo Mattia.

He's the first one to hug me, and I return it because, over the years, he's become the closest thing to a human connection I have to my grandfather. He's taken me under his wing and didn't stop pushing me to the top until I reached where I am now.

"*Ben fatto*, Valentina! *Ben fatto*," he says and taps the left side of my helmet as he continues to throw more praise my way. He urges me to keep going to celebrate with my team, too. Scarlette hugs me tightly, patting my back while we tell each other how proud we are of one another.

And I thank her for everything she's done to get us this title because I'd be nowhere without her.

I'd be nowhere without a lot of people, which is something I continue to realize as I hug every mechanic and engineer from my team who has come onto the track to celebrate this victory with me. Even some of Adrian's people are there for me, which makes sense because at Velocità Rossa, we're all one big family.

And the Italians certainly know how to celebrate better than most.

Only once I've made my way through everyone who's congratulating me do I finally move toward where the person is weighing all the drivers and then toward where they keep the towels and water bottles for the top three drivers. I down the entire bottle they gave us as soon as my helmet is off, and I love that I get to hear the people cheering for me better now.

Gabriel approaches me again once I've taken my time to soak in everything, and I fling myself into his arms. He catches me with a chuckle that I muffle by putting my mouth on his. He kisses me back fully, deeply, without hesitation, both of us drunk on the high of this moment as well as each other.

"I knew this would happen," he says after he breaks the kiss because while we may be married, and unable to get enough of each other, we're also professionals who need to give interviews. Professionals with responsibilities.

"You did. You never doubted me," I say, wiping my eyes because I need to make sure I look presentable before the interview. It's bad enough that this man with a huge camera keeps filming me from every possible, awful angle.

"Never," Gabriel replies, his dimples coming out as he smiles at me, his green-brown eyes filling with tears again. He's got those helmet lines on his face that I love with my whole heart, and when he notices me staring at his, he lifts his hand to trace mine. "It was only ever about when it would happen, not if, ma chérie," he says. "I love you so much."

"I love you the same, mon soleil," I reply, and as much as I want to kiss him again, he drops his hand when Adrian approaches to inform Gabriel it's his turn to give an interview.

My brother uses that opportunity to hug me to his side and kiss the top of my head. Now that he's not wearing a helmet either, I can see the tear tracks running down his cheek. He did his best to get rid of the evidence, but he's my brother, so I'd be able to know if he was crying whether he tried to hide it or not.

"You've been crying," I point out as I lean into his embrace.

"Shamelessly, because I've never been prouder. Plus, you should know by now that your dreams have always meant just as much to me as my own, if not more, and seeing you accomplish the very thing that you've always dreamt of? Yeah, I'll be crying for the next few weeks, Val. Try and stop me."

"I don't want to stop you. I'll cry with you. We just probably have to get ourselves a few boxes of tissues then, especially because Gabriel is going to be crying with us." My brother bursts into laughter, but he slaps a hand over his mouth to keep from interrupting Gabriel's interview.

All amusement leaves me when I see him.

James approaches me, wearing jeans and his team shirt now, and I'm a little scared he's going to hate me forever, even if I did nothing wrong during my race. I'd be lying if I said that, had I made a mistake that cost me my own race, I'd still be pissed at the person who won instead of me.

But James is a good person, he always has been. That's why he hugs me tightly, telling me he's so proud of me, before leaving again. He doesn't linger, which tells me he is hurting right now, so I don't ask him to stay for another moment either. Anyway, I have no time to because Cameron approaches me to wrap me up in a bear hug.

"You fucking did it, Val. You are the champion of the bloody world. I'm so proud of you," he says and kisses my cheek, a very wet kiss that has me giggling and wiping my cheek. "I love you," he calls out before jogging away.

I'm still laughing when it's my turn to be interviewed.

And I couldn't be happier to see Hana Yoon, the woman who interviewed me after my first win in F1. The motorsport legend.

"You've done it, Valentina Romana. You are the World Champion," she says, and I can't fight the tears that shoot back into my eyes.

The only reason they don't drop is because I notice Gabriel scrunch his nose, clearly offended she didn't say both of my last names, especially because she did for him. Gabriel Romana-Biancheri.

"Tell me, how does it feel?" Hana asks, and I focus entirely on her as I answer the question as honestly as possible.

"Surreal. Like someone walked past me down the street and told me I was World Champion. I can't quite believe it, so it hasn't sunken in just yet," I admit, which the crowd takes as a sign to cheer even louder for me, probably to make it feel real to me. It works a little, if I'm being honest.

Hana goes on to ask me a few more questions about the race itself until eventually she says, "One last thing, Valentina. I think everyone is desperately hoping for another inspirational speech of yours. Do you have one to give?"

I think for a moment as a nervous laugh skips past my lips, and it's the sight of Adrian and Gabriel giving me encouraging looks that have me speaking before I can overthink my words.

"My grandfather used to say, 'You can give up if you want, you can throw it all away and pretend your dream never existed, but if you clench your teeth, scream at the top of your lungs, and go through with it, you will end up more than happy with yourself.' So, that is what I did. I clenched my teeth, I screamed at the top of my lungs, and I kept fighting. And I wish I could tell him that he was right. I wish I could tell them that fighting for what I wanted, for my dream, has made me more than happy with myself."

Sharing this part of my life, a piece of my grandfather, with the world makes me feel closer to him in a moment when I wish he could be here to hug me, to see that his dreams for me have finally come true.

It may be the exhaustion, but my brain almost manages to convince me he's standing right behind Adrian and Gabriel, tears in his eyes and a proud smile on his face. I blink and he's gone again, but that single second was enough to make me understand something I didn't realize earlier.

He's here.

He's always been here, every step of the way.

He's never going anywhere.

I love you, Grandfather.

James And Estrella Go Out For Date Night

James

"I don't feel good about this," I tell Adrian, who tilts his head to the side as he frowns at me.

"This is a fantastic idea. Daisy loves me," he replies and places a hand on my shoulder as if that would comfort me at all.

"She loves you because you two have a lot in common. You're both children, except Daisy acts like an adult more often than you do." Instead of being offended, my best friend bursts into laughter, bending at the waist and never letting go of my shoulder, no matter how hard he laughs. "Adrian, I'm not joking. I'm genuinely concerned for my daughter's well-being," I say, but he still finds this nothing but amusing. "Usually, your wife is here to supervise both of you, and that was the deal for tonight as well."

"Well, my wife—" He cuts off for a second to grin at those two words. "—is busy tonight trying to get an article written." He turns around and walks into the kitchen of my house, and I follow him because he keeps talking to me, the jerk. "Don't worry. Nothing is going to happen to your little princess. We will have some homemade pizza, play some games, watch a movie, and then I'll tuck her into bed. It'll be a chill evening," he promises, but no part of me believes he wouldn't give her three tubs of ice cream to devour, which would ultimately result in her having a stomach ache.

Also—

"*Homemade* pizza? As in you're cooking?" Adrian nods, and pure dread fills me. "Okay, I'm calling this off," I announce and attempt to make my way toward where Estrella is getting ready in our bedroom when he catches my arm to stop me. He opens his mouth to say something, but I beat him to it. "You almost burned down your kitchen a few months ago attempting to make *soup*," I remind him.

"The key word here is 'almost,' James. Come on. Val taught me her recipe, and I wanted to share it with Daisy." He gives me his version of puppy dog eyes, blinking rapidly to sell them even more.

"Can't you just order in?" I plead, which brings back his brilliant smile.

"It'll be fine," he assures me, dragging out the word 'fine' to make me feel more settled.

I don't.

The doorbell rings, pulling me out of my conversation with Adrian. I leave him standing in the area between the living room and kitchen, walking toward whoever is behind my front door.

Never in a million years did I think it would be Chiara with Leonora and Kireran by her side as well as Leonard, Gabriel, Val, Cameron, Storm, and Scar.

"Oh, thank God," I say, my head dropping in relief.

"Nevaeh called us and said Adrian would be watching Daisy by himself, so we all sprinted to our cars to get here," Val explains as she walks into my house without waiting for an invitation.

"You've got to be kidding me," Adrian says, and I would look at him if I wasn't so distracted by Leonard's little smirk and the fact that I'm watching eight more members of my family strolling into my house, all of them here to take care of my daughter.

"How did they convince *you* to come?" I ask Storm in Spanish because he's the last one to make his way over the threshold.

"Scar promised me we were having dinner. She didn't tell me we'd be having it with everyone," he explains, scowling as always. It makes me chuckle.

"I would have understood one more person, but all of you?" I hear Adrian complain, but I don't pay him any attention.

I can't.

Not when my wife walks out of our bedroom in a short, light green summer dress that complements her curves and the warm brown color of her skin. She's put on makeup that has her hazel eyes practically shining, and she painted her lips in a dark red that makes me want to have her kiss me all over so she puts her lipstick stain everywhere.

She's twisted her brown hair into a crown braid, several pieces not incorporated in order to hang loosely around her face, framing it.

In other words, Estrella looks devastatingly beautiful, and my breath has officially been knocked out of my chest.

The gravitational pull my little star has on me makes me close the distance between us at the same time she walks toward me. She's not even the slightest bit surprised by everyone being here, which tells me she's probably the one who called Nevaeh, worried about Daisy, too. As much as we both love Adrian, he's a bit of a menace.

"Darling, you look incredible," I say, digging around in my pocket to pull out the pair of earrings I bought her for tonight.

"*Gracias, mi amor. Tú tambien*," she replies, taking the earring box from me to open the lid and reveal a pair of earrings in the shape of popcorn, matching where the theme of our date tonight. "*Me encantan*," she says and pulls them out before putting them on.

"*Y tú me encantas*," I reply, which has her grinning and blushing in response.

I bring my hands to either side of her face, leaning down to kiss her lips when she places her fingers on my mouth.

"I know what you're trying to do, but I've just spent ten minutes making sure this lipstick is perfectly in place. I won't have you smudge it," she says with a little smile, and I almost groan against her fingers because I want to kiss that smile.

I want to kiss her.

"Fine, but later, I want at least a dozen lipstick stains all over me." Wrapping my fingers around her wrist, I pull her hand away from my mouth to lean down and kiss her cheek instead. "Sound like a deal?"

"Sounds like we won't be watching much of the movie," she says and giggles, taking my hand in hers to lead me toward the door. "Which is fine by me. I'm not wearing any underwear for that very reason."

Bloody hell.

I clear my throat as I follow her out the door, throwing a quick "Thank you!" over my shoulder for my friends.

Then, Estrella and I are finally alone for the first time in weeks.

I love being a father, but I also love being a husband, and sometimes, with all of our responsibilities, it's hard to remember to prioritize both of these titles at the same time. I know Estrella struggles with the same thing, which is why I asked Adrian and Nevaeh to babysit in the first place.

So we could have an evening just for the two of us.

We drive an hour to France for the newest location of a Drive-In Theater that they've built there recently. We stop at a burger place for dinner, but we take it to go since we're in a rush to actually make it to the drive-in before the film starts.

We sit and talk almost the whole drive, trying to catch up with each other because even though we live together, both of us have been so tired recently, that whenever we get to bed, we simply fall asleep. We don't get to share what's happened in our day. We don't get to spend time in each other's arms. No. We only get to sleep, and then we're not even very good at that because whenever work calls her, she answers. And I'm travelling for the F1 season, so I don't get much sleep either, trying to get to my flights on time.

So, we talk. The entire time. Without any periods or commas.

We only stop once we find a spot at the theater, and I park my car where we can perfectly see the movie. There's not going to be a single other person here for this showing because I bought all of the tickets, which means Estrella and I are all alone to do whatever we feel like doing.

Especially because I bribed the employees with some paddock passes so they leave us alone, too.

I rented a big SUV so we could have lots of space. But that also means that once we get out of the car, I tell her, "I need you to face the screen for a moment and don't look back until I'm ready for you to." Estrella furrows her brows in confusion.

"Why?" Unable to help myself, and because her lipstick is mostly gone now after eating, I place my lips on hers instead of answering.

I trail kisses from her mouth to her ear.

"Because we're going to have some fun while we watch the film, and I'm going to make sure we're comfortable and hidden throughout." I kiss a trail back toward her mouth, kissing her longer and harder.

I shouldn't have kissed her at all.

It's like a person who's been starving for weeks finally getting a taste of food again, unable to stop themselves from eating until they feel full.

Except I don't feel full at all. I've been starving for Estrella for weeks, and part of me is contemplating forgetting about the cute setup I had planned to simply take her back into the car and slip inside her until we're both no longer hungry for each other.

"James," she says, her voice low to remind me that we're here to watch a movie.

"Yes, you're right." I place one more kiss on her mouth, making her giggle, before turning her to face the screen.

Estrella doesn't say anything at first while I set up, but I notice her looking around, noticing that there are no other cars anywhere near us.

"Tell me you didn't buy every single ticket for this showing," she says with a shocked laugh because I don't have to answer her question.

She already knows.

"Then what would you like me to tell you, little star?"

"Does that mean I get to be as loud as I want to be?" she asks, which makes me chuckle as I finish setting up the pillows.

"No, darling, you'll still have to be quiet because there are people who work here that, while they promised to leave us alone, could still hear you if you're too loud," I remind her, and I can almost see her pout.

I can most certainly hear it in her voice.

"Fine."

I approach her once more, slowly turning her around to show her the way I've set up the trunk of our rental. I placed sheets down, then added half a dozen fluffy pillows, a thick blanket, and as many snacks as I thought she'd want.

Estrella studies the setup with her hand lifting to her mouth, and I wait patiently beside her to find her words again.

I just didn't expect them to be what they are.

"Screw the movie."

Her fingers dig into the front of my shirt before she pulls me to the trunk, pushing the snacks aside while dragging me on top of her. Her mouth moves back onto mine, and I let out a surprised laugh. Then, I kiss her back just as fiercely, enjoying the way her dress rides up to reveal that she wasn't lying.

She's not wearing any underwear.

"You're a threat to my health, Estrella," I say because of the way my heart is racing and how lightheaded I feel since all of my blood has rushed south to make my bulge press against her bare pussy.

"And every centimeter of you could be the cure to all my aches," she says, her head dropping backward as I run my tongue down her neck.

"Every centimeter?" I ask with a smile.

Estrella reaches between us, cupping my groin and forcing a groan out of me as pleasure consumes every part of my body.

"Yes, sir. Every centimeter," she replies as she palms me, almost making me come in my pants.

"On your side, wife. Let me take care of your aches."

Her answering giggle has my chest expanding and pulling tight at the same time, but she obeys quickly, tilting her head to make sure she can still kiss me while I pull down my pants and position myself behind her.

"I love you so much," she says, lifting her hand to my nape.

"In every galaxy," I reply before losing myself in her.

Chiara and Leonard Take Leonora and Kieran Strawberry Picking

Chiara

Mamma and Nonna have been keeping my children so busy all week, I've hardly seen them. On one hand, it's allowed me to look after my gallery here in Italy to make sure everything is running smoothly. On the other, I'm missing my babies, and I wish my family would stop hogging them.

Not that I can blame them.

Mamma hasn't been to Monaco in months, so she hasn't seen her grandchildren for as long. Nonna has never been to Monaco or England, so she only gets to see her great-grandbabies whenever Leonard and I bring them to her. It's been almost a year since we've taken a family trip down here because of how busy we are with our jobs and careers, so it's long overdue.

"Little demon, are you almost ready to go?" my husband asks, and I can't help but grin as soon as his voice travels through our room and reaches the bathroom.

"Yes, *amore mio*. I'm ready now," I say as I apply my perfume, the one he bought me years ago because he thought it matched me so well. He buys it for me now every single time he notices my bottle getting low, and I even catch him sometimes sneaking it away on business trips when it isn't fully empty yet just so I can be with him in a way.

He appears in the doorframe of the bathroom, and I watch him approach me in the mirror right up until his arms wrap around me from behind. Then, my eyes fall shut as I enjoy his embrace the way I always do when he hugs me.

His arms are so strong, his touch so safe, I could fall asleep immediately with his body enveloping mine.

Life has been extremely tiring recently. I've been taking on too much with all of the different art gallery locations, being a mom, and trying my best to also be a hundred percent present in every aspect of my life.

The only reason I haven't crumbled under everything is currently hugging me, keeping me together.

"You look stunning, sweetheart. Truly breathtaking," Leonard says as he kisses my temple, his arms still around me like two steel bands.

"Thank you," I reply and open my eyes again to see his brown ones studying me in the mirror. "My husband has good taste," I add because he bought this dress specifically for today.

It's blue and has strawberries woven into the design at the straps of the dress and the hem of it. It also has a corset-style upper half that's pushing my boobs up wonderfully, showing them off to Leonard.

Noticing where my attention has drifted to, he lifts his hands to cup my breasts before running them down my upper body, resting them on my hips. He places his chin on top of my head, smiling and showing off his perfect set of teeth.

His perfect smile.

"If I had even better taste, I'd have gotten you nothing and told you to wear that." I elbow him in the side, and he starts laughing at his own comment. "You can't blame me. I may be a big fan of fashion, but there is not a single piece of clothing in the world more beautiful than your naked body."

He goes back to hugging me, and I do my best to keep my heart from palpitating at his sweet compliment.

Having two babies changed my body a lot. I have even more stretchmarks than I did before, I have a c-section scar from Kieran's birth, my boobs are even more uneven too, and I have more cellulite. But I'm so comfortable in my own skin because my husband *worships* me. There are days he spends kissing every inch of my body while he tells me exactly why he loves that part. He has never, not once, made me feel insecure about the changes. If anything, he spends more time making sure I know how gorgeous he thinks I am.

Then he thanks my body for giving him the two greatest gifts in his life.

"We should go. Leonora and Kieran were practically bouncing off the walls from excitement when I told them we were going strawberry picking," Leonard says, and I turn in his arms to pull his head down and kiss him.

"Then let's go," I reply, but he kisses me again. And again. And again. Until I'm giggling in his arms, true happiness consuming me.

Leonora and Kieran are sitting on the couch with Nonna, listening to her talk about Nonno. They never got to meet him, so she tries to keep his memory alive by telling the youngest members of our family about him. Mamma did the same thing when I was a kid, sharing stories about her grandparents with me.

My precious little girl is glued to Nonna's every word while Kieran, who is clearly too young to understand much of what she's saying, is playing with the toy his daddy bought him yesterday. It's a toy car, the same model that Leonard drives nowadays: a Grenzenlos H3. He may have not finished his F1 career in a Grenzenlos F1 car, but he never gave up his private Grenzenlos sports car, not that they made him.

Grenzenlos will probably continue to sponsor my husband until the day he dies, especially now that he's thinking about getting back into Formula One, even if it's not as a driver but as a team principal.

A decision he's meant to have made by the end of the month, and not even I, the person he confides in about everything, know what decision he will make. Because he doesn't know yet, or if he does, it's a decision he must have made within the last twenty-four hours.

He can't keep anything from me for longer than that.

"Did you put them in matching outfits?" I ask Leonard when we reach the living room and I notice both Kieran and Leonora are dressed in blue pants and shirts the same color as my dress with strawberries drawn on the front of their tops.

"Obviously. Didn't you notice my outfit?" he asks, and I step back to look at him. He's wearing a polo shirt the same color as our outfits, and white shorts with a single strawberry on his pockets.

"We're taking pictures, aren't we?" I say, and Leonard moves toward where his bag is in the entrance to pull out the Polaroid camera he bought me all those years ago.

"Of course we are."

I shake my head and chuckle because all of this is just so Leonard.

I love it with my whole heart.

***

Leonora and Kieran are having the time of their lives. They never leave each other's side, and today is no different. They walk down the rows of strawberry plants, leaning down together to inspect each individual one. They have little meeting type of conversations about each strawberry before deciding whether or not to put it into the basket Leonard is carrying for them.

"This is why I can't decide what to do," Leonard says, dragging my attention from our kids and straight to his handsome face.

His indecisiveness is written all over his face, and I reach out to take his hand in mine as we continue strolling through the field, following our children.

"I know." I squeeze his hand. "I know they're why this is so difficult for you, but, Champ, they'll always have you around. If it's a little less, they will get used to it. You will get used to it. And with my galleries taking off, I can hire more staff. I can travel the world with you more, taking the babies with me. If this is what you want to do, all you have to do is say the word."

Leonora and Kieran stop walking, so Leonard does too. He uses the opportunity to twist me his way, looking deep into my eyes as he considers my words.

Processes them.

Thinks about them.

"Becoming team principal would be a dream come true," he admits in a whisper, ensuring our children don't hear him.

"Then take the job, Leonard. Stop torturing yourself. We will adjust to this as a family, just like we adjusted from having one child to having two. That was a wonderful change, and this can be too."

Before I know what has hit me, his arms wrap around me and he pulls me into a tight hug. He holds on for a long moment, needing this comfort to allow himself for the first time in months to let the possibility of things turning out okay no matter what he decides to sink in. He needs me and no one else right now.

It's a heady feeling to be so loved by your husband, even after a decade of being together and almost as long of being in a marriage.

"Thank you for making this easier."

He kisses me, but it's a brief touch of our lips. Brief enough so our kids don't have to be weirded out by us, a fear Leonard and I share. We try to keep a good balance between making sure they know how much we love each other and grossing them out with too much touching and hanging onto each other.

"Thank you for giving me a life like no other," I reply as we turn to look at our children again.

"That's my line," he complains playfully right before Leonora interrupts our conversation.

"Daddy, give me the basket. We found a perfect strawberry," she says and wiggles her fingers at her father to get him to move. He's so wrapped around her little finger, he obeys immediately, leaving me to watch after him with the biggest smile on my face.

Sneak Peek of Saved by His Halo, The Pitstop Series book #8

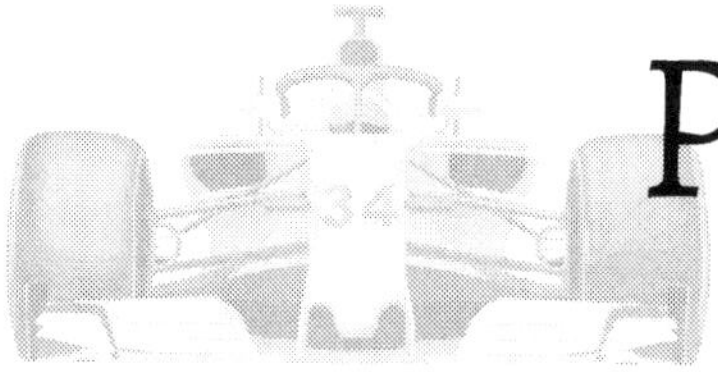

Prologue

Cameron

Picking up the pieces of a shattered heart is a lot more difficult than people lead you to believe. Especially when you were planning to marry the person and spent almost half a decade with them by your side, talking about your future. Especially when they cheat on you with the one person they always assured you meant nothing to them, that they were no one you had to worry about.

A tear drops down my cheek as I take a sip of my coffee.

Maybe it's wrong to be drinking coffee at one in the morning, but if I don't have a cup, I'll fall asleep, and I'm having a hard time sleeping at the moment. Being in our bed without him brings me too much pain to handle, and even when I finally allow myself to try and sleep, it's always on the couch, far away from his scent. Not that I sleep much or for long because the nightmare of Elijah cheating, the image of them naked in bed with each other, haunts me in my dreams, too.

Although it's completely dark out and I can't see a thing, I stay on my porch and keep my eyes trained on my family's ranch. It's December here in Australia, and I'm enjoying the warmth of the summer temperature even this late at night.

I close my eyes, holding the mug with both of my hands as I listen to the nocturnal wildlife around me make all sorts of noises.

Another tear drips down my cheek.

No part of me understands how he could do this to me, to us. We wanted to get married. We were planning to adopt a child. We wanted *everything* with each other.

Now we have nothing left.

Nothing but pain.

More tears follow, so I cover my face with my hand, sobbing into it.

I've never felt anything like this. I've never felt so betrayed, humiliated, torn into a million pieces, and enraged at the same time.

He sat next to me, his arm wrapped around my shoulders, kissing my temple as he whispered, "It's you and me against the world, Ronnie. You're everything to me. I'll never need more."

My sob turns into an unamused laugh.

He really fooled me with that bullshit.

"Cami?" My sister's voice travels from the front door all the way to where I'm sitting on the wooden bench to the left of it, and I quickly wipe my tears before she appears in front of me.

"Hey, Hazelnut," I reply as she stands in front of me with her arms wrapped around herself. Hazel is only twelve, but we've been through enough in this family for her to often act like she's an adult already. She's certainly had to be with parents like ours. "Why are you awake, honey?"

"I had a feeling you might need me," she replies, and I feel my heart warm as her words sink in.

"Come here," I say and open my arms after placing my cup of coffee to the side.

She studies my face with her brown eyes for a moment, narrowing them as if she knows something's wrong with me.

My heart palpitates in fear because I don't ever want her to be able to pick up on that. My sister shouldn't have to worry about me.

"You've been crying," she points out but also closes the distance between us so she can sit on the bench beside me while I wrap my arms around her.

"I'm having allergies," I lie, but my sister snorts because we both know that is the lamest thing I could have said. "Yeah, I've been crying, but it's okay. Even broken hearts mend over time. I just have to be a little more patient with mine while it stitches itself back together." I kiss the top of her head and hold on tighter, feeling a bit of the pressure that was weighing on my chest easing because she's here with me.

She's easing my pain, and I can't help but hold onto her.

"Maybe you can help stitch it together," Hazel says, and I tilt my head down to look at her.

"How?"

She doesn't know Elijah cheated on me. I've kept that secret from my siblings, but she does know that we broke up. Telling both of my sisters that the guy they saw as another older brother would no longer be around destroyed me all over again, but they were kind enough not to ask more questions when they realized I didn't want to talk about it.

"Find something or someone else to fall in love with. A heart can't be broken if it's too busy fluttering in excitement every time you see it or them," my sister, the future poet, says with a gentle tone.

The very thought of falling in love again turns my stomach upside down, but falling in love with some*thing* turns it the right way around again. Hazel has a point, and I squeeze her arm a little as I let my mind wander.

Hazel rearranges next to me until she's hugging me from the side, her head resting on my chest. We don't speak again, but her words swirl around in my head, trying to turn what she said into the solution to my problems.

There's only so much time I have in my life between being an F1 driver, taking care of my family, and trying to spend time with the family I found over the years. It was one of the reasons why Elijah said he cheated on me. Because I had no time for him. Because I was always busy working. Because he felt like what I was giving him wasn't enough.

There's nothing like being told you're not good enough right after you catch the man you thought was the love of your life with his hand wrapped around another man's dick.

I suck in a silent but sharp breath to keep the tears away and since her head is on my chest, Hazel notices and holds me tighter.

"You'll be okay, Cami. Elijah was not the man you were meant to spend the rest of your life with. He was a singular chapter in your story, and now you can flip the page and write the next one."

"You really are going to be an author one day, aren't you?" I ask Hazel as I kiss the top of her head again.

"Yup, and I'm going to write about your life. It'll make for a great book."

I tickle her side until she's laughing so hard, I can't help but join her.

She's right.

It's time I write the next chapter of my story.

To be continued...

Saved by His Halo

Coming in 2025

Translations

Mijo, te ves muy guapo - My son, you look very handsome.

Gracias, Mamá. Tú también. - Thank you, Mamá. You do too.

Quiero ser tu todo, arcoíris, para siempre. - I want to be your everything, rainbow, forever.

Hermano. - Brother.

Hola, mi querida esposa. - Hello, my lovely wife.

Puñeta. - Fuck..

Tiene sentido, mi arcoíris. - That makes sense, my rainbow.

*Siempre tengo sentido, mi amo*r. - I am always right, my love.

O puedo hacerte venir ahora. - Or I could make you come right now.

¿Estás escuchando? - Are you listening?

Entiendo todo. - I understand everything.

Entiendes todo o escuchaste todo? - Do you understand or did you just listen?

Cual es la differencia? - What is the difference?

Tú eres mi vida. - You are my life.

Te quiero mucho, arcoíris. - I love you very much, rainbow.

Te quiero mucho, arcoíris. Con todo mi corazón. Con todo lo que tengo. - I love you very much, rainbow. With all my heart. With everything I have.

Te quiero más, mi amor. - I love you more, my love.

No es posible, esposa. - That's not possible, wife.

Quiero que vengas gateando hasta aquí, mami. - I want you to crawl to me, mamí.

Hola, Julián. Es un placer volver a verte. - Hello, Julián. It's a pleasure to see you again.

El placer es mio. - The pleasure is mine.

¿Quieres ir conmigo, mi arcoíris? - Do you want to come with me?

A donde? - Where to?

Dime, mi amor. Sé que quieres decirme algo. - Tell me, my love. I know you want to tell me something.

Arcoíris, ¿dónde estás? - Rainbow, where are you?

Puñeta, esa mujer me tiene loco. - Fuck, this woman is driving me wild.

¿Qué quieres, mami? Hmm? - What do you want, mami? Hmm?

Tú ganaste, mi amor! - You won, my love!

No, arcoíris. Nosotros *ganamos.* - No, rainbow. *We* won.

Gracias, mi amor. Tú tambien. - Thank you, my love. You as well.

Me encantan. - I love them.

Y tú me encantas. - And I love you.

About the Author

Bridget L. Rose is a queer author currently located in Toronto, Canada. She was born in Germany and is half-Italian and half-German. During her teenage years, she was fortunate to live in Singapore and the USA as well.

Bridget fell in love with books from a young age, and soon discovered her passion for writing as well. Over the past two years, Bridget has written and self-published ten books. She writes contemporary romances, most of them set in the world of Formula One. Her first cowboy romance will be releasing in April 2025.

In her books she aims to be inclusive because of her own experiences of being queer and living with mental illnesses. Even nowadays, people still make assumptions and use stereotypes about queer people as well as people with mental illnesses, which she experiences daily as well. Bridget is passionate about changing the narratives on these subjects, especially in the romance market.

When Bridget is not busy writing, she loves to read and spend time with her family, including her two furry children JJ and Diego.

Books by Bridget L. Rose

The Pitstop Series

Jump-Start

The Inside of a Rainbow

Rush: Part One & Two

Chase: Part One & Two

Reserved

Diffuse

The Last Championship (Novella)

Straight to the Chapel

Silver Creek Ranch Series

To Pluto & Back

From Angels to Devils Series

From Devils to Angels

Printed in Poland
by Amazon Fulfillment
Poland Sp. z o.o., Wrocław

54357030R00129